I0234592

CHALLENGES
of
GOVERNANCE

CHALLENGES
of
GOVERNANCE

An Insider's View

B.K. CHATURVEDI

RUPA

Published by
Rupa Publications India Pvt. Ltd 2019
7/16, Ansari Road, Daryaganj
New Delhi 110002

Sales Centres:
Allahabad Bengaluru Chennai
Hyderabad Jaipur Kathmandu
Kolkata Mumbai

Copyright © B.K. Chaturvedi 2019

The views and opinions expressed in this book are the author's own and
the facts are as reported by him which have been verified to the extent possible,
and the publishers are not in any way liable for the same.

All rights reserved.

No part of this publication may be reproduced, transmitted,
or stored in a retrieval system, in any form or by any means,
electronic, mechanical, photocopying, recording or otherwise,
without the prior permission of the publisher.

ISBN: 978-93-5333-450-5

First impression 2019

10 9 8 7 6 5 4 3 2 1

The moral right of the author has been asserted.

This book is sold subject to the condition that it shall not,
by way of trade or otherwise, be lent, resold, hired out,
or otherwise circulated, without the publisher's prior consent,
in any form of binding or cover other than that in which it is published.

Dedicated to
Riya, Dhruv and Nikita

CONTENTS

PREFACE

When I thought of writing about my experiences as a civil servant, it was clear that in a long working life, choosing some events over others was going to be a difficult task. I was also constrained by various decisions taken in complete confidence. It is not for a civil servant to reveal what is said in trust. To many people having retired from the service, this may not be relevant. But I consider trust sacrosanct. This has precluded me from mentioning several things to which I was privy as Cabinet secretary or in earlier assignments.

Before undertaking this book, I was plagued by conflicts. Should one write memoirs at all? Are they of any value? Do these meet any need, except to perhaps satisfy the intellectual needs of the author? There is a school of thought that such documents do not fill any gap in the field of public administration, as situations change with time—how does it matter how certain problems were handled in the past? But I have reflected on this and rejected this view. It is important that civil servants write about their work and the manner in which they met the challenges. This is the material from which learning evolves. These events make us think about current situations, when issues of public governance arise. The idea behind writing this is to reconstruct events. This is how future historians will work. If all civil servants were to keep quiet and pen nothing down, it may be a dark period in our history of public governance.

This book is about my experiences as Cabinet secretary and later as a member of the Planning Commission. But in writing about them, I have referred to my background as well. The book involves a brief mention of the early years of my life. I have started with my early education and how I joined the civil services. There is also a more detailed description of my work in the districts and later in some of the key assignments as secretary to the Government of India. The intention was to lay the background for readers to understand the experience that one brings to a crucial job like that of Cabinet secretary.

The institution of Cabinet secretary has evolved primarily after Independence as a successor office to the secretary, executive council of the viceroy of India from the British times. Its present location in the Rashtrapati Bhawan complex is a remnant of that era. Later, the powers of the council were exercised by the Union Cabinet when Independent India adopted its new Constitution. The Cabinet secretary in the initial four decades enjoyed extremely wide-ranging powers. With the setting up of the institution of the national security advisor (NSA), these have been curtailed. I have tried to deal with this transition and also with the dynamics of power-sharing between the Prime Minister's Office (PMO) and the office of the Cabinet secretary, both of which work under the prime minister (PM). It is often not realized that the Cabinet secretary has no substantive department allotted in the allocation of business rules. Even the departments under the PM are handled by the respective secretaries, who send papers directly to him.

So the Cabinet secretary's primary work includes advising the PM on issues of governance and resolving interministerial differences. I have also dealt with the problems faced by coalition governments in providing good governance. Considering the federal nature of our polity, this is a serious issue.

I worked as a member of the Planning Commission for seven years after completing my term as Cabinet secretary. This gave me the opportunity to look at a range of developmental issues. I have, therefore, devoted two chapters to my work in the Planning Commission and on related issues. While doing so, I have dwelt extensively on the widely discussed reports of the Comptroller and Auditor General (CAG) on the 2G spectrum and on coal-block allocation, as these, in my opinion, laid new ground rules for the working of the institution. There is a large body of persons that has appreciated these documents, with many believing that it has helped reveal large-scale corruption in the system. I do not agree with this view. It is important for our institutions to work in the framework of the Constitution and evolve healthy norms to which they can stick, and all corrupt acts must have some quid pro quo. I have serious reservations about the approach adopted by the CAG in his report, where he has practically appropriated the right to frame government policies and then gone forward with estimating the losses caused to the public exchequer. Dishonest acts, given the large-scale corruption in our society, need to be identified and punished. But one must clearly identify the corruption flowing from abuse of office for private gains, as is the globally accepted approach. The report of the CAG has led to the start of a judicial process where ordinary administrative decisions, if falling foul of prescribed guidelines, have been treated as criminal acts. This has weakened the ability of civil servants to take risks and focus on achieving results for the benefit of the people, and has adversely impacted day-to-day governance. It has promoted inaction. The current approach has obliterated the distinction between honest civil servants and a large body of dishonest functionaries. I feel concerned about this.

During my work, there were occasions of intensive interaction with the PM and ministers. At several places in the book, I have given the gist of the conversations.

The epilogue raises a number of issues related to public governance that I consider important for our nation's rapid development in future. There are, however, areas that I have deliberately posed as questions and to these I find no good answers.

Chapter 1

A SURPRISE SURVIVAL TO SUCCESS

I began my journey in this world from a humble town called Karwi in the erstwhile Banda district of Uttar Pradesh (UP). At the time of my birth, the stars were not very propitious. All the pandits who reviewed the alignment of the heavenly bodies when I was born felt there was very little chance of my survival unless my parents performed a special puja. My father was only a sub-inspector in the police then and was busy with his academic pursuits. He was doing his Master of Laws (LL.M.) from the Allahabad University. Though himself a very knowledgeable astrologer, he told my mother—as she mentioned to me later—that he had no money for the sort of puja the pandits wanted and that 'if he is destined to not survive, so be it'. But despite the doomsday predictions, I did survive.

My earliest memories include travelling to primary school in a bullock-driven 'school bus' and studying there while sitting on the floor on a *tat patti*, or a handwoven carpet. Starting out, we would write on slates with wooden pens dipped in liquid chalk. From these humble origins, I moved to other schools in the state, owing to my father's transferable job. After completing my Class XII, I moved to Allahabad University, considered the Oxford of the East, in the late 1950s. After completing my undergraduate studies in Science, I decided to study Physics for my master's degree. However, I was not very happy with my results and decided to switch to Political Science. This subject was popular and substantially covered the course in five papers, in which candidates had to compete while appearing for the Indian Administrative Service (IAS) examination—one of the primary reasons why so many of us came to Allahabad, a city known to provide a large number of candidates for the All India Services (AIS) in those days. But this change was short-lived. Very soon, I got offers for teaching assignments, and joined as associate professor of physics in the engineering college in the city. However, I did appear for the IAS examination as well. For some reason, many of the top positions in the IAS were invariably from Allahabad University. So when I took the examination, I was certain of being in the first few. In those days, the names of the first ten positions were announced on the radio. My father listened carefully when the results were declared. But he was very disappointed—my name was not in the first ten. It was, in fact, a few ranks below. For him, it was a failure.

Working in UP

I joined the UP cadre of the IAS in 1966, and after a year's training in Mussoorie, got posted in the state. UP then included Uttarakhand. Politically, it had been the centre of the freedom movement and a powerful influence at the Centre. In terms of population, it was, and still is, the largest state in the country, and had some of the finest service officers.

I started my service as an assistant magistrate in Bareilly. This was where Vibha and I got married. Bareilly was a thriving town in western UP. After the initial familiarization with the functioning of the district administration and training in Land Records at Hardoi, I moved to Ranikhet, which was part of Almora district in the Kumaon hills, as the subdivisional magistrate (SDM). Ranikhet was about an hour and a half from Almora town. There were very few roads in the area and the mode of mass transport was bus. The revenue administration in rural areas had police powers and forest panchayats managed large tracts for the welfare of the village community. It was a challenging job to be the SDM of this vast hilly area. A year later, I was called to the Lucknow secretariat in the Ministry of Agriculture.

After spending more than two years in the ministry at the state secretariat, I was posted as the district magistrate (DM) of Azamgarh*; even at that time, it had a huge population of 27 lakh and fourteen Assembly constituencies, or 3–4 per cent of the entire state, which had nearly fifty-five to sixty districts at that time. Poverty in the district was high, even by eastern-UP standards. Surprisingly, people took pride in the fact that the Patel Commission, set up to identify backward and poor districts, had named Azamgarh too. Some of the people were so poor that they would consume gubraila, a part of cow dung. But widespread

---

*Azamgarh is now a divisional headquarters, with three districts—Azamgarh, Ballia and Mau—as part of the new commissioner's division. Mau is a new district carved out of old Azamgarh.

poverty was just one of the major challenges—communal violence and natural calamities, including floods and droughts, would often wreak havoc on the district.

When I joined as DM in February 1973, against the backdrop of communal riots in Sajni and Nonari villages, a judicial enquiry was ordered. At that time, polarization between the Hindu and Muslim communities was high. Very soon, I realized that to instil confidence in the minority community, particularly in the large concentration of Muslim weavers in the Mau and Mubarakpur towns, I had to build bridges with them.

I noticed that the district had a tradition of holding mushairas, or poetic congregations, in different towns, organized primarily by the minority community. So, to begin with, I decided to accept their invitations and attend all mushairas, which gave me an excellent platform to interact with many minority community leaders. This confidence-building was further strengthened by another incident within a month or so of my arrival. One day I was informed that in the village of Hamidpur, efforts had been made to burn the crops of some Muslim cultivators. I promptly rushed to the village and ordered action against the miscreants. It had a salutary effect. Riots in rural areas had to be stopped right from the first instance, as it would become difficult later, because we did not have the police force to send to so many villages. This approach helped us later, when communal riots flared up in Azamgarh town during the Holi and Milad-un-Nabi festivals in March 1975. We were able to control the riots effectively, and there was a lot of support from both communities.

The district had a history of both drought and flood in different parts. I witnessed this within a few months of my joining, when we were hit by a severe drought. This was a recurring phenomenon; the district had very limited cultivable tracts under irrigation and it did not have a good canal system then. The Sharda Sahayak network of canals was still under construction; and the tube-well irrigation system was inadequate and needed expansion. Within a year, there were floods too. The flooding was due to Ghaghara, Tons and some other minor rivers. Several of these would normally be dry but overflow their banks in the rainy season as they drained into the Ganga, which would also be in very high spate during the rains. Also, drainage in many parts of the district was very poor. In many low-lying areas, habitation and cultivation had begun due to increasing population. All this contributed to the flooding of large tracts of land and habitation.

The recurrence of natural calamities had given rise to a dependency syndrome. People looked to the government during such problems, and when relief was late or inadequate, there was massive criticism. So I decided to focus on developing underground water, getting electric connections to tube wells for all those who applied, and working on the early development of the canal system. I wanted to rapidly expand exploitation of underground water to improve protective cover in times of drought and bolster agricultural productivity to increase incomes. There was also an effort to grow high-income-yielding crops, especially bananas and spices. The expansion of rural development programmes was closely monitored. The procurement of wheat went up during this period, as productivity increased due to strong focus on making fertilizers available in time. With the support of the state and Central governments, we were able to set up a cooperative spinning mill for producing yarn near Maunath Bhanjan, a sugar factory in

Sathiaon village to process cane into sugar and a chilling plant for processing milk collected from cultivators.

During State Assembly elections I witnessed the extent to which political rivalry could go. The district had a strong presence of Opposition parties, including the socialists. PM Indira Gandhi was scheduled to address three meetings—in Mau, Mohammadabad Gohna and Azamgarh town. While preparing for these meetings, we received an intelligence report that members of one of the Opposition parties had sinister plans to disrupt Indira Gandhi's public meeting at Azamgarh town. The police worked on this input and, finally, a day before the meeting, took a local leader of a Socialist Party into preventive custody. He was upset and said that we would soon understand the gravity of our actions when 'snakes and scorpions' came out. We dug deeper, only to find that a plan had been hatched to release scorpions at that public meeting. The meeting was scheduled for the night and the ground was not large. If this were to happen, many lives would be lost in the stampede. We finally arrested a 'Musahar'*, who was supplying frogs and other animals to the laboratories of some schools for their studies in biology. The leaders had paid him money to get the scorpions, which had been kept in a small mud receptacle. However, he was not aware of the reason for this.

In January 1974, less than a year of my joining the district, a movement was launched in Gujarat against the government of Congress Chief Minister (CM) Chimanbhai Patel. Students joined

---

*Musahar is a poor community of eastern UP, Bihar and other eastern parts of India. It is believed that in old times, they would trap rats and eat them. Now members of this community are often engaged as artisans and village labourers for agricultural work.

the state-wide protests against price rise and corruption. Within two months, a similar movement was launched in Bihar. All the political parties in the Opposition came together and sounded the call for a revolution. They asked all Members of the Legislative Assembly (MLAs) to resign, and people were told to stop paying taxes. The Hindi newspaper *Aaj*, which was widely read in Azamgarh, provided news of various developments in the adjoining state of Bihar. People in the district had traditionally very close interaction with the neighbouring state. This fuelled prolonged agitation and processions in some parts. In view of the inflation and the shortage of essential commodities, small incidents gradually assumed larger proportions. We informally kept in touch with local leaders to ensure peace. Both the senior superintendent of police (SSP) and I had excellent relations with all political parties, and many of them were aware of our fair dealings. This helped enormously in maintaining peace and avoiding violence during this difficult period.

A Dark Era

The Bihar movement, popularly known as the JP movement after veteran socialist Jayaprakash Narayan who led it, ultimately resulted in tough countermeasures by the Central government to curb widespread lawlessness. In the second week of June 1975, Justice Jagmohan Lal Sinha of the Allahabad High Court, in a judgement, held the election of Indira Gandhi as member of the Lok Sabha void and found her guilty of corrupt practices under the election law. He also debarred her from holding any elected office for six years. In her appeal in the Supreme Court (SC), Justice V.R. Krishna Iyer allowed her to continue as prime minister but did not permit several privileges as a Member of Parliament (MP). J.P. and other leaders now intensified their agitation. A national Emergency was declared on 25 June 1975. I recall getting a wireless notification from the state government about the promulgation of the Emergency. But I was not very clear about its implication. We could anyway arrest miscreants and people disturbing peace. Soon, however, there was extensive screening by the police of various individuals, especially those belonging to banned organizations. Several people, including Ram Naresh Yadav, who later became the CM of UP after the elections in 1977, were arrested. The JP movement had now faded away. The agitations were practically over. There was an atmosphere of fear. There was noticeable improvement in employees' discipline. There was great improvement in the availability of goods, with curbs on profiteering. Prices were under control. Absolute power in a democracy leads to tyranny, causing the harassment of innocent people. The Emergency was a dark era.

I left the district on a new assignment in Lucknow as director of information in mid-1976. I was subsequently given a state award by the government for my outstanding work in the district.

Allahabad

I spent nearly five years in Lucknow on several assignments. I was suddenly called by the chief secretary in February 1981 and asked to take over as DM Allahabad. The previous incumbent had been transferred after communal riots in the town. When I reached the city, the tension between communities had already subsided substantially. The district held special significance for the state government, since the CM, V.P. Singh, had his constituency in the district. I stayed there for just seven months. Since I had studied and taught there, settling down did not take much time. During this short stay, I had to conduct the annual excise auction, in which liquor shops were allotted. The auction was always conducted under the supervision and presence of the DM. That year, I conducted the excise auction and got an extraordinarily high bid. It was accepted, but the bidder did not deposit the money. So another auction was held and, this time, we got a good bid in the open auction but lower than the earlier one. As the presiding officer, I asked the final bidder to raise it further. He did so and we accepted it. The bids were to be finally approved by the excise commissioner. But the government intervened and ordered a fresh auction. The bidder went to court. When the CM came to Allahabad the next time, I met him and protested, 'You have made both you and the government look good, but have put a question mark on my reputation, which I value highly.' He mumbled something to the effect of 'you know what Allahabad is like' but had no real answer. There was, however, no rancour on my part, and he respected me for it. Finally, at a later date, when the Allahabad High Court decided the issue, my decision was upheld and the government's order set aside.

Though short, Allahabad was a satisfying stay for personal reasons. When in service, my father was posted in the district as the deputy superintendent of police (DSP) and oversaw the functioning of the administration. He was keen to see one of his sons become the DM of the district. This was an opportunity for me to fulfil his wish. He stayed with me during this period. However, within less than two months of my transfer, he died.

I have always treasured this tenure as special in my entire career.

Lucknow

I moved back to Lucknow in September 1981. Over the years, I had four stints in the state capital. During these I worked on several assignments, as deputy secretary (agriculture), director (information), administrator of the Lucknow municipal corporation and secretary to the government of UP in various departments, including appointments, general administration, power and institutional finance and banking. Interestingly, I also worked with V.P. Singh as director (information) and secretary of the department during this period. My move to Delhi was a result of this last assignment, though I worked on this only for a few months before things changed.

One afternoon, as I was in Delhi for a meeting, I got a message that the CM had resigned. I had no inkling of this, though I was in close touch with him. I got to know that some scheduled caste families had been attacked near Kanpur and had succumbed to their injuries. Taking the moral responsibility for this, the CM sent his resignation to the governor. When I reached Lucknow, he saw me and remarked, 'So the Director missed the biggest news today!' As he was demitting office, he called me and enquired whether I wished to go to any other job in the state. I politely declined. 'What can I do for you, then?' he asked. I mentioned to him that I was keen to go to Delhi but was not sure how I could get a decent assignment there. I also requested that the position of director be taken away from me, as I wanted to move on. He agreed. He took out a small diary and made a note. The very next day orders were issued that left only small departments in my responsibility.

For the next year and a half, I must have received several calls from the former CM. One evening as I was having dinner, I got a call. 'Chaturvedi, I had been trying to speak to a few ministers, including Pranab Mukherjee, about bringing you to Delhi. But nothing happened. Today I have taken over as commerce minister. Tell me when you can come,' V.P. Singh told me. It took me about six months to move to my new assignment in Delhi.

Delhi

On my first stint in Delhi, I joined as executive director of the Trade Development Authority (TDA) in February 1984. This was an organization under the Ministry of Commerce. In about a year, I moved to the ministry and worked for five years during one of the most momentous times in our history. I used to handle trade relations with east European countries. The emergence of Mikhail Gorbachev and the transition of the USSR to a free market economy were taking place at that time. Other east European nations—Romania, Poland, Yugoslavia, Czechoslovakia, Hungary, East Germany and Bulgaria—were also undergoing economic reforms. Gorbachev had referred to this as perestroika (reform) and glasnost (openness). However, this era of transformation was not without hilarious stories of change, as narrated to us by former Soviet trade negotiators during our interactions. Under the communist regime, prices of various items were fixed by Gosplan, the planning commission of the Soviet Union. It did so for millions of items. As the system moved to market pricing, they were in a fix. There was no market in existence there. The concept of market players competing with one another and thus determining the market price was alien to their economy. So when I enquired about how the prices were being fixed in the changed conditions, one of the trade negotiators jocularly remarked, 'We have adopted the system of ceiling prices now. We look at the ceiling and fix the price!'

There was a massive shortage of goods in this phase. One did not know which item would be available in the market when. It was possible that one would go out to buy eggs and return with a refrigerator. The transition of the Soviet Union to the open-market economy had other consequences too. In the next decade, the Soviet Union broke up, followed by Yugoslavia and Czechoslovakia.

Interestingly, another powerful communist nation, China, under Deng Xiaoping, had started reforms in 1978, earlier than the Soviets, and brought in many pro-market ideas in the economy. They managed the transition far better than the Soviets.

When I was nearing the completion of my term, T.N. Kaul, our ambassador in the USSR, asked me to join him in Moscow in the embassy. He was believed to be very influential, because of his close family relationship with the then PM, Rajiv Gandhi. He tried very hard but was not successful in getting me to Moscow. The PM did not agree to relax any rules. In the summer of 1989, I moved back to Lucknow and was asked to join at Nainital.

Nainital

It was a homecoming of sorts when I reached Nainital to take over as commissioner of the Kumaon division.

While I focused on several projects for economic growth in the region, including the supply of drinking water, promotion of tea cultivation, expansion of small industries and improvement of horticulture, three developments on the national front had a significant impact on administration in the division during this period. First, the Ram Janmabhoomi dispute picked up momentum, leading to a yatra in several parts of the state. This was a potential point of tension in the division, as these processions passed through various districts. Later, when firing took place in Ayodhya on some kar sevaks, things got even more serious. The leaders of the movement, including Professor Rajendra Singh (Rajju Bhaiya), were sent to a forest rest house in the foothills to be detained. Second, with a large number of Sikh settlers in the Terai region of the division, Sikh terrorist activity continued to be strong. This required continuous and close watch. Third, there was agitation for setting up a separate state of Uttarakhand. Students were a part of this and, at times, it was difficult to maintain public order with a small number of policemen and a hilly terrain, in which managing a stone-pelting crowd was difficult. In early 1991, CM Mulayam Singh Yadav resigned after losing the Assembly election. I moved to Agra as commissioner shortly after that.

Agra

While I had not worked earlier in the region, my ancestors were all from here, and settling there was easy. The division had its headquarters in Agra and had six districts as part of it: Agra, Firozabad, Manipuri, Frah, Mathura and Aligarh. The CM, Kalyan Singh, was from Aligarh and had his constituency in that district.

After about a year and a few months, the Ayodhya issue heated up. On 6 December 1992, the Babri Masjid was demolished. This was a trigger for possible rioting between Hindus and Muslims. Home secretary Prabhat Kumar (who, about a decade later, was appointed Cabinet secretary in the Government of India) telephoned and discussed the possibility of repercussions in my division. The division had a large Muslim population and very high communal sensitivity. All the districts had a history of communal riots. There was another cause for worry. Earlier, political groups had raised slogans that the Krishna Janmabhoomi Temple Complex, Mathura, could be next on their agenda. This now appeared a real possibility. We were worried that large-scale rioting could be triggered by this event. There was insistence from Lucknow to hand over the complex to the Army. But it had implications, as the station commander, Mathura, insisted that no one but a magistrate on duty would be allowed to enter the complex for prayers. Hari Paliwal, the DM of Mathura at that time, felt that such restrictions would start a new conflagration. Finally, we strengthened security at the complex and did not hand it over to the Army. We used the Army columns for a flag march to strengthen the security environment. While all district officials were kept on alert, I toured the entire division, along with the deputy inspector general (DIG) of police. Except a few small incidents, there was general peace after the Babri Masjid demolition. Kalyan Singh, who had assured the highest court of the safety of the mosque, had to resign and President's rule was imposed on the state.

Delhi Again

While I enjoyed my work in UP, I was keen to move to Delhi again. I was looking for avenues and decided to apply for the position of chairman of the State Trading Corporation (STC). It was a very senior assignment, but with faster promotion in the state,

I was eligible. It was purely fortuitous. Later, after my selection by the Public Enterprises Selection Board (PESB), the Ministry of Commerce wanted me to get absorbed in the STC and resign from the IAS. I had rejected this idea five years back and saw no reason to change my view now. The ministry was, however, adamant and did not wish to recommend me for the job unless I agreed to absorption in the STC and severing my relations with the IAS.

One evening I got a call from A.N. Varma, the principal secretary to the prime minister. We had worked together in the Ministry of Commerce when he was the commerce secretary. He asked me for how long I wished to go on deputation to the STC, to which I replied, 'Three years.' He advised me to pack my bags and be ready to move quickly. It seemed that the government had decided to exempt me from the absorption rule for the next three years.

I joined as chairman of the STC in October 1994, which was engaged in making large-scale imports for the government of a variety of commodities, including sugar, fertilizer and palm oil. It also had an export portfolio, though not of its own products. At times, the government would advise it to make imports from the international market to improve domestic availability and ensure moderate price levels. But they were not willing to bear the risk of losses, if any, in the operation. This debate would at times spill into the public domain, leading to a surge in prices, as India was always a very large buyer. So when finally the imports were made, it cost the government a lot of money and losses. Before I joined, this had happened in sugar imports, with huge problems for the consumers. I tried to rectify this approach in the imports of wheat and sugar with moderate success. However, while pushing our exports, my experience during this period was that there was massive corruption in many South Asian and African countries, and large agent commissions were required to bag export contracts, and at times to even get payment for the goods exported by us. To me agent commission is often a euphemism for bribery and corruption.

I stayed in the STC for three years. While my tenure was coming to a close, I fell out with the minister who wanted to promote a particular group in our purchases. He was also upset with me for not having disclosed in advance my wheat-import plan. I requested the Cabinet Secretary T.S.R. Subramanian, for a change. The STC was a very stressful job, but there was one lesson I learnt there that has stayed with me all my life: 'Never try to take the market for granted.'

Reforms

India was still in reform mode in the '90s, and was considering opening up the insurance sector when I joined the Ministry of Finance in 1998 after finishing my tenure in the STC. There were six government companies engaged in the insurance business at that time: Life Insurance Corporation (LIC) of India, and five others in general insurance. There was strong opposition from them to the introduction of private insurance companies in the country. They were worried that their business would be taken over by the new private players. Many political parties, too, were opposed to it. They argued that private insurance companies would not bring any new technologies and, rather, take away huge profit from the country. Insurance was generally considered a very profitable business. While our government-owned companies were doing reinsurance with international firms, the original insurance was of only these companies.

All the industry and business organizations were strongly in favour of opening up. They argued that insurance companies rarely repatriated profits, as they were interested in expansion. They gave the example of Unit Trust of India (UTI), which was government-controlled, and after the opening up of the mutual fund industry where private players had set up funds, there had been a massive increase in the size of the market. A similar increase was expected here. The Congress, though in opposition, was supportive of the move. I briefed Dr Manmohan Singh, who was leader of the party in the Rajya Sabha then.

LIC prepared well for the coming change and continued expanding business even when the private sector joined the competition. The general insurance companies were not ready for the competition and faced problems when private players started their operations. My experience during this entire period was that with the regulator on insurance talking the same language as me, there was never a false step. The government cannot speak in different voices and hope to keep a public policy well understood. Very soon opposition to this decision dissolved. We were able to get the amending legislation through the Parliament, and I had the satisfaction of seeing the first private-sector insurance company start business in India.

I joined as secretary in the Ministry of Human Resource Development (HRD) in 2000. The ministry's policy required focus on women and children, improving literacy levels and reforms in the quality of education. An initiative which needs special mention is the constitutional amendment to declare the right to education as a fundamental one. The issue had been pending for some time and there was reluctance to move forward. I recall our briefing deputy PM L.K. Advani on it, following which the proposal was brought before the Cabinet. There had been reports that implementing it would be costly. These must have reached the ears of PM Atal Bihari Vajpayee too. So when the issue came up in the Cabinet, and the then minister for HRD, Dr Murli Manohar Joshi argued for it, PM Vajpayee commented that it was difficult to fund it. After some discussion, this Cabinet item was fixed for consideration at the next meeting. Sometime in 1993, the SC had given a ruling that the right to education was inherent in the right to life guaranteed by our Constitution as a fundamental right under Article 21. Next time when the item came up in the Cabinet, it was passed without any discussion. Later, the constitutional amendment was moved in the Parliament, and much later an Act was passed on this issue.

I moved to the Ministry of Petroleum and Natural Gas after HRD. Several reform initiatives taken at that time proved to be critical for our economy. The most important of these was to release the oil prices from government control and allow oil companies to fix the price in accordance with market conditions. This also entailed the entry of the private sector in the marketing of petrol and diesel. The Oil and Natural Gas Corporation (ONGC) and other oil producers got in the bargain international market prices for the crude oil which they were supplying to domestic refineries. This freedom has been restricted by the government on umpteen occasions, especially when oil prices have been high in the international market or when elections are round the corner. A sharp rise in oil prices caused massive problems in managing the economy in the United Progressive Alliance (UPA) years. But the reform was vital for the growth of the sector.

I would also like to mention an important initiative taken at a critical time, which helped turn around Mangalore Refinery and Petrochemicals Limited (MRPL). The refinery was running at a loss and needed additional funds every month. The market indications were that an asset worth ₹9,000 crore would be sold to private parties for about ₹60 crore. This was unacceptable to me. I discussed this with the oil companies. Subir Raha, chairman of ONGC, showed interest. But it was an upstream company in the business of exploration and production of oil from the oil fields and not in processing it to produce petrol, diesel and other products. They were, however, able to find a provision in their article of association which permitted this activity. And they bought MRPL. Today, it is a thriving refinery with high profitability.

While MRPL was an important initiative, a project that had far-reaching implications for the economy and the energy sector related to liquefied natural gas (LNG). LNG is, in fact, natural gas which is converted to liquid form by cooling it to very low temperatures. This makes it possible to transport it over long distances via cryogenic ships. In 1998, public-sector oil companies— the Indian Oil Corporation (IOC), Bharat Petroleum Corporation Ltd (BPCL), ONGC and GAIL—set up a company called Petronet LNG, with the secretary of the petroleum ministry as its chairman, to provide natural gas in the Indian market. A French company, Gaz de France, was its strategic partner. Petronet later signed an agreement with RasGas, Qatar, to provide LNG for twenty-five years. It, however, had a clause under which, if we did not lift the LNG, we would be liable to pay huge penalties. Once in India, the LNG was to be stored in specially designed vessels near the sea and gradually reconverted to natural gas in the LNG terminal being built at Dahej, Gujarat. This gas was then to be transported through the pipelines already laid out and distributed to the customers.

When I joined, I found some diffidence in the oil companies, as they were not sure that their investment would give reasonable financial returns. To turn around the project, I took three decisions. First, I decided to cut project costs and bring about a change in the project parameters without impacting efficiency. Second, I renegotiated the price of LNG being imported from Qatar. Third, I looked for wider possibilities to sell LNG in our domestic market.

For funding, I approached the Asian Development Bank (ADB) to invest in the project. The public issue was a huge success. Both these sources gave us adequate funds and helped us in the efficient completion of the project. Today, the project is supplying about 40 per cent of gas supply in the Indian market. The share price of the company has gone up by more than twenty times over the past fifteen years.

Chapter 2

APPOINTMENT OF A CABINET SECRETARY

I t was the summer of 2004. I had been working as secretary to the Government of India in the Ministry of Petroleum and Natural Gas. It had been more than two years and I was due to bid goodbye to the government in a few months. With experience of more than a decade in the energy sector in different capacities, I was planning to look for a teaching post on my superannuation in July that year. Around the same time, elections to the Lok Sabha had been announced and it was generally believed that the National Democratic Alliance (NDA) would come back to power again.

One of the most powerful and effective persons in the government hierarchy then was Brajesh Mishra, principal secretary to the PM. A man of few words, any matter referred to him got a quick, decisive response. Sometime in early May 2004, I called on Mishra with respect to an issue about the Ministry of Petroleum when elections were on. He advised me to come after about a fortnight—by which time the new government would be in office—and said he would sort out the issue then. I decided to wait. It was clear that the NDA government was returning to power and Mishra would continue as before.

Pollsters had predicted a comfortable win for the NDA, which had been able to win several Assembly elections only some months back. The government had decided to call for early elections. It was proud of its work and the running a campaign of India Shining. The government was not in the grip of any corruption scam and PM Vajpayee was generally liked across the political spectrum.

But the election results confounded all political pundits. The NDA lost. Many said that rural India did not vote for it. Interestingly, the PM had started a scheme of rural roads, which was an unmitigated success in terms of connectivity and providing opportunities for a larger income. The cess on petrol and diesel had helped build national highways across the country.

When the election results were announced, I was leading a delegation at an international conference in Amsterdam, the Netherlands. The results meant that our delegation in Amsterdam was caught in a transition phase. We, however, continued with our presentations at the conference. In the meanwhile, the new UPA government had been sworn in and Mani Shankar Aiyar was given the charge of the Ministry of Petroleum. I had known him in passing earlier in the '80s when he was working with former PM Rajiv Gandhi. I rang him up to extend to him a warm welcome to the ministry and regretted that I was not present in New Delhi myself. He responded that we would discuss everything when I was back.

I landed in Delhi the next day. The new minister was very much in the saddle. As a former foreign service officer, he had extensive knowledge of international issues.

A critical issue that needed early resolution was the sharp rise in crude oil prices in the international market in early 2004. Within a short time, it had risen to $35 per barrel, as against $28 only a few weeks back. We were importing crude oil from abroad to meet more than 70 per cent of our requirements, processing it in our oil refineries and producing a range of products, including petrol and diesel. The domestic prices of these products thus moved in sync with the crude oil. Since the government had decontrolled the oil sector about two years back, oil companies were now changing prices of petrol and diesel every fortnight to keep these aligned with international market prices. In actual practice, they consulted the ministry informally before changing the price.

The adjustment in the petrol and diesel prices was an unpopular decision for the new government. Having taken over the reins of office only a few days back, the government was reluctant to start off on this anti-consumer note. The new minister would sit down every morning and discuss various options for fixing prices so as to avoid volatility and increase in prices. He was clearly not enamoured of the prevailing system for fixing petrol prices and termed it the 'Ram Nayak pricing method'. Ram Nayak, the petroleum minister in the preceding NDA government, was consulted informally before oil companies, like the IOC, announced revised prices for the next fortnight.

On one such afternoon, after the discussion on finding a new method for fixing petrol and diesel prices was over, I mentioned to the minister that if the new government was thinking of appointing a new Cabinet secretary, I was one of the three from the senior-most batch. I understand the minister mentioned this to the PM, Dr Singh. There was, however, no indication that there would be any change, as the serving Cabinet secretary had a term until October 2004.

New Appointment, New Challenges

On a very hot summer day in June, I got a call from the PMO that the PM wanted to see me. I was not sure what the agenda was. Dr Singh was a polite man and asked me about my views on governance and the administrative reforms required. I mentioned various measures but focused on the declining standards of honesty in the service, especially in the people's eyes. There was a clear need to revive the integrity of the system. We discussed it more and he thanked me. After a few days, he called me again. He wanted to know whether I had enough time left before superannuation. I had then only about two months before I was to retire. He discussed about the current senior-level secretaries working in Central ministries and devoted some time to various ideas on administrative reforms needed to change the system of governance. On 11 June, I was informed that the PM wanted to see me immediately. Dr Singh again asked me a few questions and then announced, 'I have decided to post you as my Cabinet secretary. Please take over charge of your new assignment.' I thanked the PM and assured him that I would try to live up to his expectations of providing good governance. After some time, Kamal Pande, the serving Cabinet secretary, was ushered in. The PM told him about the change in his assignment, and he was later moved to the inter-state council. He was clearly upset. His tenure was until October 2004 and it was being cut short. As I reached my residence, I found that Sanjaya Baru, media advisor to the PM, had sent a senior journalist to speak to me. Things were happening at a fast pace.

Under the current AIS rules, some are tenure posts and officers work on it only for a prescribed period—generally two years—irrespective of the date of retirement. This decision now enabled me to work in this new appointment until June 2006.

I had never worked with Dr Singh in any capacity prior to this. I later learnt that he had met about ten senior officers, including those he knew personally, whom he thought could be considered for the post of Cabinet secretary. In seniority, there were two other officers ahead of me. He had made very thorough enquiries about me before finally making up his mind. This made my job more difficult. I had to live up to a higher level of expectation.

Generally, as a good governance practice, a new Cabinet secretary is always first posted as officer on special duty (OSD) for about a fortnight. During this period, he sits in various committees, along with the outgoing Cabinet secretary. This ensures a smooth transition. With the change of government and its decision to go in for a new incumbent, this did not happen with me. I took over as the new head of the civil services the very next working day.

Setting Up an Institutional Selection Process

There is no specific procedure laid down for the selection of a Cabinet secretary. Generally, the outgoing incumbent sends a note, after considering which the PM takes a decision. The selection procedure adopted in my case was not the usual one. Dr Singh, who interviewed several officers of the senior batches, including me, and then made a selection, gave up this procedure later. In a few years, he had come to know all senior secretaries, and hence did not need to interview them afresh. The next two appointments of Cabinet secretaries were done without any interviews, as I learnt from service colleagues.

In United Kingdom (UK), a new incumbent is selected based on the advice of the outgoing Cabinet secretary and the first civil service commissioner. In India we do not have any office which performs the function of first civil service commissioner. The selection and posting of the Cabinet secretary has always been done by the PM, who chooses from the senior-most civil servants of the IAS. Generally, one or two senior batches are considered. From that the choice is generally confined to the senior-most five or six officers. All officers who reach this level usually have an excellent service record. The choice quite often is based on the nature of experience and the type of jobs held. The wider the variety of jobs done at senior levels, the better the chances of being selected as Cabinet secretary. There have, however, been occasions when the choice of a new incumbent has not been very transparent.

The selection process for choosing a Cabinet secretary needs a change. We need an institutionalized arrangement as part of the professional service tradition to ensure that the appointment of the senior-most civil servant of the country is not governed by political manoeuvring. I would, therefore, suggest that we have a settled policy under which the PM should take the advice of the last two Cabinet secretaries before making up his mind about a new incumbent.

The role and function of the Cabinet secretary also needs a relook. It has to be appreciated that the institution of the Cabinet secretariat was created primarily for secretarial functions, including organizing Cabinet meetings and maintaining its records. Later, many functions were added to it. It now provides coordination among departments when there are differences, and is often the originator of new policy initiatives. It also performs monitoring functions, especially when prices rise and policy intervention is required. It keeps the president, the vice president and the prime minister informed of major developments.

With corruption seeping in through all tiers of the government, one of the issues that need a closer look is that of the members of the council of ministers adhering to the code of conduct prescribed to them. This has become extremely important as probity in public life has become the avowed objective of most political parties. Since the PM must keep a close watch on it, this function needs to be fulfilled by the Cabinet secretary. This will improve probity in public servants too.

From Shastri Bhawan to Rashtrapati Bhawan

I took over my new assignment the next day. I was sad that Kamal decided not to come to the office for a formal handing over of the charge. I moved from Shastri Bhawan, where the Ministry of Petroleum and Natural Gas was situated, to Rashtrapati Bhawan, in whose campus the Cabinet secretariat is located. I had time for a short meeting with the staff. The Petroleum Minister, while happy at my elevation, also remarked that it was unfortunate that his secretary had been transferred in only fifteen days of his joining. I was, however, pleasantly surprised to read a news item in *The Times of India* captioned 'An Officer and a Gentleman'.* It highlighted the

---

*Sanjay Dutta, 'An Officer and a Gentleman', *The Times of India*, 14 June 2004,

habit that my wife and I had inculcated of picking up the phone ourselves at our residence and being polite to everyone who called. In an era where bureaucracy-bashing was the norm, I thought the article was a welcome contrast.

I started my new job, however, on a completely wrong note. After taking over, I spent the next few days in office, acquainting myself with the current issues. One afternoon, the PM called and asked me to see him the next morning. As I entered his chamber the next day, he remarked, 'You have not met me in the last few days. Why are you avoiding me?' And then in a lighter vein, he added, 'I have made your selection after a lot of search.' I did not respond immediately and promised to see him the next day. I, however, clarified to him later that I wanted to see him only after a number of issues had accumulated. But he insisted that I meet him every day with a briefing on various issues. Since I did not have issues to brief him on every day, I started seeing him every alternate day. This continued for nearly three years. This was the start of a close working relationship, which continued for more than a decade, during which I worked as Cabinet secretary and then a member of the Planning Commission. I still meet him but on a social calls and mainly to ask after his health.

An important decision I had to take was whether to call on Mrs Sonia Gandhi. In my entire career in the civil services, I had been of the view that party and government were separate and that the civil services should interact only with political executives such as

---

accessed 16 March 2019
https://timesofindia.indiatimes.com/india/An-officer-and-a-gentleman/articleshow/736688.cms

---

ministers, and not hobnob with party functionaries for their career prospects. They should, thus, be completely apolitical. This was a difficult situation. Mrs Gandhi was president of the Congress party then. She was also the chairman of the National Advisory Council (NAC) and thus had the official status of a Cabinet minister. She was initially the unanimous choice for the post of leader of the ruling party but declined to work as the prime minister. This was clearly a grey area in terms of my norms. I, however, decided to call on her.

Pulok Chatterji was then working in the PMO. He had been principal secretary to Mrs Gandhi for a very long time. He was from my cadre and offered to coordinate my meeting with her. One fine morning, I landed up at 10 Janpath, Mrs Gandhi's residence. She was very gracious and welcomed me in my new assignment. I talked to her about Allahabad, a place with which her family had close political and emotional ties. I mentioned Indira Gandhi's visit to the town in the early Eighties when I was posted there as the DM. All in all, it was a pleasant meeting.

After taking over, during the course of the next week, I met all the three senior PMO functionaries. They were extremely welcoming and we discussed a few issues. It was quite clear that M.K. Narayanan, who had been appointed as an advisor on internal security matters, did not have such a well-defined role. A former director of the Intelligence Bureau (IB), he was rated very highly. J.N. Dixit (also called Mani Dixit), a former Indian Foreign Service (IFS) officer who had been foreign secretary and was highly respected for his depth of knowledge, was then the NSA and did not feel comfortable with M.K. around. I recall his mentioning to me that M.K. was very close to 10 Janpath. The problem was that the

Home Ministry looked after most of the internal security matters, so M.K. had a minimal role in internal security issues. The major chunk of security work with international implications was with the NSA. I got an impression that Dixit felt that his territory would be poached in such a situation. Dixit, unfortunately, did not live long. He died in 2005 and the job of NSA passed to M.K.

The Institution of the NSA

Until the early 1990s, the Cabinet secretariat, apart from a host of other functions, undertook coordination of intelligence obtained from the IB, the Research and Analysis Wing (RAW) and the defence forces. We had a joint intelligence committee, which was coordinated by a senior officer of the Cabinet secretariat. It thus exercised effective control over all activities related to governance in these areas, which are crucial for all nations. In 1998, the office of the NSA was created, which took over all the functions of coordinating intelligence. Mishra, who was principal secretary to the PM, took up the job of the NSA in addition to his other responsibilities. He was thus the first NSA of our country. Interestingly, several nations with our model of democracy, like the UK and Australia, created this institution later, during 2008–2010.

In all previous governments, the PM's principal secretary and the Cabinet secretary had close but often uneasy working relationships. The power centre invariably tended towards the PMO, but the nature of the Cabinet secretary's job and his personal equation with the PM often restored the balance. I soon realized that with the creation of the institution of the NSA and its being held by the PMO, the powers and the role of the institution of Cabinet secretary had further changed. Since Indira Gandhi's time, with P.N. Haksar as her principal secretary, the PMO had already been quite powerful. With the appointment of Mishra, the equation further changed significantly in favour of the PMO. As the NSA, he had wider control over the system of governance, with information from all the intelligence agencies available to him on a real-time basis. Also, he was close to PM Vajpayee. In the NDA government, however, the PMO was not top-heavy. There was only the principal secretary, who also was the NSA.

When Dr Singh took over in 2004, he felt the need for more professional advice. So he appointed three persons to share the function that was being fulfilled by Mishra—T.K.A. Nair, a former chief secretary of Punjab who was principal secretary to the PM, Mani Dixit and M.K. Narayanan. With the dilution of the Cabinet secretary's control, the incumbent's effectiveness now depended much more on his equation with the PM.

I feel that the institution of the NSA requires a relook. The expectation that internal and external security issues can be handled in a professional manner by just one person is a bit optimistic. Many of the issues related to external security require an in-depth knowledge of India's foreign relations. Internal security requires knowledge of intelligence within the country and persons who are well acquainted with working in the districts. At times, the lines get blurred when the source of intelligence is a foreign country providing some inputs on criminals operating in India. This exchange is important when we deal with international terrorists. Depending on the professional background, the NSA must have a deputy working closely with him to cover areas of expertise that the NSA may not have.

We should also place the National Security Council (NSC) organization, along with the deputy NSA who heads it, under the Cabinet secretariat. There is a similar arrangement for review by the Cabinet secretary in respect of implementation of the Chemical Weapons Convention, or CWC (an intergovernmental treaty prohibiting production, stockpiling, development and destruction of chemical weapons), and on several administrative matters of the RAW. This reform, I believe, will strengthen the Cabinet secretary's support system for inputs on these matters and help him provide more comprehensive advice to the PM on issues of national security.

Civil Service Reforms

As I settled down in my new job, I looked at how we could improve the quality of the governance structure. At the back of my mind was the question of administrative reforms, which the PM had posed to me before I had taken over office. So while I handled the day-to-day issues, this kept worrying me. I had seen over the years several changes in the civil services which were worrisome. One of the most significant developments was the erosion of people's faith in the honesty and integrity of civil servants. Some time back, two former chief secretaries of UP had been charged with corrupt acts and sent to jail. I recalled incidents from my academy days when the director, Mr Pimputkar, was reported to have let his wife be prosecuted for some minor traffic offence in Mumbai. I also recalled my initial years in service when I had suggested the cancellation of a shop's licence for selling cement on the grounds that it was charging a few paise extra for the form that each prospective buyer was required to fill and that the shopkeeper was getting printed.

As I reflected on all this, I was keen that the officers develop a strong value system.

I was also aware of severe criticism of the promotion policy for civil servants, which resulted in practically all of them getting promoted to a higher grade either at the Centre or while working in the states. This was unlike the Army, where there was a strong selection process for officers going to higher grades. Even in the private sector, there was a tough selection process. During the course of our assessment of this issue in the Cabinet secretariat, we found that the movement to the higher grades was happening in nearly all cases and was a matter of course. There were very few officers who did not reach the highest grade. There was a clear need to weed out the deadwood. Several committees on administrative reforms had suggested that after about twenty years of service, the officers should be judged afresh and those who could no longer contribute to efficient administration should be made to retire.

The short tenure of officers in different jobs was not conducive to accountability. At the Centre, it was especially worrisome at the policymaking level of secretaries to the government. In the states, transfers and postings had become an industry and a source of corruption. It went hand in hand with political patronage. Many of the systems and procedures were such that the common man could not easily get ordinary services like the ration card, a copy of his or her land records, the driving licence or an electricity connection. The methods for starting a business were time-consuming and needed to be made smoother.

I was convinced that a young civil service was absolutely necessary. It was possible for the trainers to change the mindset of the young officers and instil a strong value system in them. I noticed that once an officer got married or otherwise joined the service at a later date, his chances of imbibing a value system essential to the civil services reduced. After some analysis, we found that due to the increased age of recruitment, the average age of the officers joining the service was going up. For this, we needed to reduce the age of entry into the service. An ideal situation would be to have a maximum recruitment age of 24 years. A suggestion was also mooted at that time that we should recruit young civil servants between the age of 17 and 20, immediately after their ten-plus-two exams, and give them comprehensive training for four to five years. It would cover law, public administration and economics, apart from other disciplines. We could develop a new class of civil servants with excellent skill sets and a strong value system.

We started working on the details and were keen to move forward in the above areas. We also looked at the draft of a new civil service law. In the meanwhile, a proposal was mooted to set up a new Administrative Reforms Commission (ARC). The first ARC had been set up more than four decades back. It had been a long time and there had been many changes in the administrative environment since. So a fresh look was called for. I found there was serious opposition to my suggested direction of reforms. The net result was that an ARC was set up under Veerappa Moily, the former CM of Karnataka. Our reform proposal in the above areas was put on the backburner, awaiting the report of the commission. The final report recommended broadly the areas we were working on, apart from many others. Unfortunately, there has been very little progress in implementing the two key areas of reform we had worked on. Neither has the age of recruitment been reduced, nor are the deadwood in the service being retired after twenty years.

It seems that the idea of a new civil service law has been buried.

I was, however, able to bring about some changes, which did not get referred to the ARC. The first related to greater transparency in the system of empanelment of officers. Under the scheme of things prevalent, the Cabinet secretary used to chair a committee to empanel officers for deputation to the Central government. In this annual exercise, officers were posted as secretaries, additional secretaries or joint secretaries from this list. I felt that the committee deliberations were impressionistic and that there was a strong element of subjectivity in them. It was necessary to have a second look at the list. I suggested two changes, which were approved by the PM. As a result, the list of officers due for empanelment was initially considered by a group of eminent former civil servants, who made their recommendations. The committee under the Cabinet secretary then looked at it and prepared a panel, which was finally approved by the PM. If it differed from the recommendations of the committee of eminent persons, there had to be reasons in writing. Also, we tried to quantify the overall character roll entries of every officer over his service period. All this, along with the record, was seen before finalizing the list. I understand that the system is still in vogue, with some changes about 360-degree evaluation, and has brought further transparency to the process.

This process, however, had its limitations. There were cases where political masters got annoyed with an officer and sharply put down the evaluation in the annual confidential assessment which was the basis for empanelment in the government and further promotion. Several officers, especially from Haryana, approached me. In all such cases, we looked at the assessment of the officers during the rest of their careers and that by all other officers. Based on this and my own enquiries, I decided not to ignore officers who clearly seemed to be victims of political machinations.

The solution to the issue of long tenures of officers in assignments at senior levels posed serious problems. It was not an issue for joint-secretary-level officers at the Centre. But civil servants who were recruited initially at the age of about 24 took a lot of time to reach the level of secretary to the Government of India. As a result, most of them had tenures of about two years or less before retirement. The solution clearly was promoting them before they completed twenty-five to thirty years of service. This would ensure that they could be kept in a job for long periods. This was difficult, as there were no vacancies for promoting such officers. We tried working around it by applying stricter empanelment norms, but this had limited impact.

To supplement this effort, we identified posts that were critical for our national security and gave them two-year tenures, irrespective of their dates of retirement. As a result, we have the home secretary; the defence secretary; director IB; and secretary RAW, for minimum two-year stints. Earlier, the tenure of the director of Central Bureau of Investigation (CBI) had already been fixed at a minimum of two years, irrespective of the date of retirement.

While the Central government had a certain measure of stability, the situation in the states was bad. Transfers and postings had become the norm, with arbitrary changes in states from one job to the other at the whims and fancies of political executives. To begin with, we decided to amend the AIS Rules, asking states to fix tenures of posts and not change officers unless approved by the Civil Service Board (CSB). The process was initiated by Pratyush Sinha, the then secretary of the Department of Personnel and Training (DoPT) and later the Central Vigilance Commissioner (CVC). This issue of amending service rules lingered for a long time and no changes were made. Later, the matter went to the SC in a public interest litigation (PIL), which finally directed an immediate change in rules after considering petitions filed by a former Cabinet secretary, along with others. The changes were made in the rules after the SC order in 2013. The states have, however, still not implemented this policy, as there is strong resistance from the political dispensation. It is unfortunate that instead of focusing on policy formation, many ministers have chosen to devote their energy to transfers and postings.

I would often attend celebrations at the residences of service chiefs and was impressed with the pride our armed forces have in their work and what their men have done for the nation. Increasingly, I got convinced that the civil services needed to celebrate some of its excellence in delivering public services and to remind themselves of their capabilities and reinforcing their commitment. This had to be linked to a leader who had been an icon for many in the field of public governance. Sardar Patel was an obvious choice. We realized that his speech to IAS probationers of Independent India would be a good starting point. So we chose 21 April as Civil Service Day. The PM approved the proposal. The first celebration was in April 2006. Subsequently, we decided to give awards to civil servants or their teams that had done outstanding work. Gradually, it has become more professional and is now a two-day affair.

Civil service reforms require a clear direction and a strong political will to disturb the status quo and usher in new institutions. It needs a bureaucracy that is committed to the directions of change. I do not support the view that a comprehensive report should be first prepared before embarking upon such reforms. It must be a continuing process but with strong political support. It is often argued that a coalition government is not in the best position to take tough measures. Considering that major economic reforms in the last three decades have been implemented by such governments, I find no reason why key administrative reforms cannot be made by them.

Managing Key Appointments

As the secretary of the Appointments Committee of the Cabinet (ACC), one of the key responsibilities of the Cabinet secretary is selecting officers for senior-level positions, including the foreign secretary, the chiefs of Army, Navy and Air Force, director IB, secretary RAW and a host of other appointments. He chairs a number of selection committees for key appointments in the security establishment.

The selection of most officers was done on the recommendations of the CSB, which was presided over by me. The board generally made recommendations from a list prepared by the DoPT. We would meet every Monday for the purpose. But ministers were not very happy with the process.

After a couple of such meetings, one minister complained to the PM against me, stating that his suggestions to include the names of officers for posting in his department were being ignored. I explained that the lists were prepared based on the names thrown up by the computer on the basis of experience. There was a heated discussion at the Cabinet meeting. The PM later discussed the issue with me and observed that apart from other names, the suggestion given by the ministry should be considered too.

As a matter of practice before posting secretaries in the ministry, I would invariably consult the concerned minister and have a panel. Many of the ministers were new or had come into the government after a long time in the Opposition. They did not have any idea about the officers. It was not very difficult for me in the initial few months to make changes even at senior levels. Increasingly, it became more difficult. Often, I would consult a minister and tell him the best choice for him. Usually, they would agree. At times, one or two very senior ministers, who were initially very punctilious, wanted to see the full professional details of the officers. As the years passed, the choice of officers by ministers started having greater weightage. Normally, I would consider this a good development, where a leader wants to select his team to deliver results for the public good. Unfortunately, the selection of officers or a recommendation for it by the minister was considered quite often by the civil servants as a favour. With a high level of corruption prevalent in the system, there was the danger of civil servants being soft during crucial decisions. This was not good for governance.

Postings of officers at times pitted me against some important ministers. Let me narrate two instances that highlight the need to protect officers from political pressures. Handling these is especially difficult in a coalition government. The first incident relates to the posting of a member in the railway board. Those days (I understand the system is broadly the same even now) the proposals for the appointment of a board member were sent to the Cabinet secretariat after the approval of the railway minister. The person being proposed for the appointment had to fulfil certain norms. In the instant case, the Railway Ministry wanted to bypass a certain officer, even though there was nothing against him on record. I modified the proposal and, based on this, the ACC, which included the home minister and the PM, approved the name of the officer that I had sent. When this news reached the Railway Minister, he was furious. I was at my residence when the minister called. He mentioned that I had posted a very close relative of a prominent Opposition politician of Bihar as member of the railway board. He added that it was not the correct decision and that I was advising the PM wrongly. He also remarked that if I wanted to continue this way, I should run the railways myself.

I talked to him politely and explained that the officer had been posted in accordance with the rules. I further added that the Cabinet secretariat did not keep a record of officers' relationships with politicians, which was, in any case, irrelevant to these assignments. I also pointed out that since he was the railway minister, it was his responsibility to run the railway system. Our conversation ended with this rather factual response from me. Shortly thereafter, I briefed the PM on this and pointed out how the Minister was trying to bypass the norms. I did not hear from the Minister again on the issue. The officer whom we had recommended joined as a member, though with a delay of two or three months, as another vacancy in the board was to be filled in a month or two. But the interesting thing was that the next time I met the Railway Minister at Cabinet meeting, he was cordial and showed no rancour.

The second incident relates to the posting of an officer as the chairman of the National Highway Authority of India (NHAI). We had posted the officer a month or two back when the Minister for Shipping, Road Transport and Highways complained to the PM that the officer was not working well and should be shifted. I called the chairman of NHAI and ascertained the facts. It seemed that the minister wanted a certain officer, who was an engineer, to work in the personal office of the chairman. The chairman, who was himself an engineer from IIT, did not feel the need for this input. I briefed the PM with the full facts of the case and pointed out that the officer had been posted only in consultation with the minister, and that he was happy with the choice. Considering the emphasis of the government on infrastructure and the need to give long tenures to officers, this seemed an unreasonable request. It seemed that after sometime, the minister again reminded the PM about it, which was duly conveyed to me. The minister did not want to give in. I found approach unfair and against all norms of good governance. I advised the PM to ask the minister to discuss the issue with me. From then on, for the next four or five months, the minister would raise the issue with me with great regularity. I could see that coalition partners were trying to embarrass the PM. So whenever the minister would give me a ring, I would mention that the matter was being processed and whenever a suitable vacancy would arise, for which the concerned officer was a good choice, I would suggest his name for that new assignment. The minister was upset and complained against me. But I did not permit any change until the end of my term.

Over the years, I have seen a strong desire in political executives to select officers they think will do their bidding. This focus on personnel rather than programmes does not improve governance. Sadly, there seems to have been no change in this approach.

Chapter 3

COALITION CONUNDRUM: TRIALS AND TRIBULATIONS

D r Singh's Cabinet was formed on 22 May 2004, but not before great drama. After the Lok Sabha elections, the UPA, led by the Congress, formed the government. Mrs Gandhi, who was the chairperson of the Party and had led it to victory in the elections, was the natural choice for PM. When the Congress Parliamentary Party (CPP) meeting took place to select its leader, almost every MP spoke in her favour. But she was reluctant to take oath as the PM. Finally, it was decided that Dr Singh would be the choice of the Party for PM. With huge administrative experience and his past tenure as finance minister, where he had earned high praise for ushering in economic reforms in the country, Dr Singh was highly respected. But he had practically no political base. This arrangement, however, where political power rested with someone other than the PM, especially in a coalition government, later gave rise to certain problems. A major weakness of the coalition was that, of the 272-plus votes required by the UPA government to win a vote of confidence passed in the Lok Sabha, the UPA alliance of the Congress and like-minded parties had the support of just 218 MPs. The majority in the Parliament was feasible only with outside support. The Communist Party of India (Marxist), or CPI(M), along with other like-minded parties, had fifty-nine, the Samajwadi Party (SP) had thirty-six and the Bahujan Samaj Party (BSP) had nineteen MPs. Government formation was feasible only with the support of these parties. This implied a major say of these parties in governance, even though these were not part of the government. So when the government was formed, it had a weak structure and was dependent heavily on outside support. To enable a more principled support, a common minimum programme (CMP) had been agreed upon, which provided common ground to parties with diverse philosophies to justify coming together.

Initially, Dr Singh's council of ministers had sixty-seven members. This included twenty-eight Cabinet ministers and thirty-nine state ministers, with ten having independent charge. Of these, a major share was of the Congress, with forty-two ministers, followed by the Rashtriya Janata Dal (RJD) with eight, the Dravida Munnetra Kazhagam (DMK) with seven, and others about one to three. With the support of the CPI(M), the SP and the BSP, though they were not a constituent of the UPA, the government could claim a backing of about 330 MPs of the Lok Sabha in a house of 543. When I joined as Cabinet secretary, the new government was barely three weeks old. Several new ministers were yet to appoint their private secretaries and other staff. While some of them, who were regular employees of the Central government, joined their new assignment quickly, there was difficulty with the others. The ministers wanted, at times, to appoint officials in their personal staff who were employed elsewhere. It was necessary to see that the new employees were security-cleared by the IB and that their former employers had relieved them for deputation to the Central government. This took some time, as the deputation process had to be completed. But the ministers invariably wanted their entire team to start working straightaway and not wait for any security clearances.

Cabinet Formation and Expansion

The settling down of the council of ministers was, however, smooth, except in a few cases. These required my personal intervention. Of these, the most interesting case was that of the minister for textiles. He had an IAS officer working with him without even being on Central deputation. This was a clear violation of rules. The minister felt particularly upset that he was not able to choose him as part of his team. He felt it was a downgrading of his powers from his earlier stint as CM of Gujarat, where his orders were obeyed by all. It was with great difficulty that I was finally able to resolve this issue during a breakfast meeting with the minister. I explained to him that the officer concerned could not be part of his office as he was not on Central deputation. The process was to be finalized by the DoPT and the state government. It took some time before all the processes were completed. The officer, however, did not get his salary during this time.

While participation in the Cabinet meetings was generally confined to Cabinet ministers only, there were some special invitees too. The Central government had a number of ministers of state—including those of civil aviation, women and child development, and urban poverty alleviation—who were allocated departments on an independent basis. In all such cases, they were entitled to taking decisions on various issues of their ministry or department, unless the matter required Cabinet approval. An invitation to participate in Cabinet meetings was extended to them when proposals concerning their departments were being considered for decision. They were also asked to join when the Cabinet was considering proposals concerning some other department but which would have implications for their own. Often, ministers of state would ring me for such invitations, pointing out the implications of certain proposals. In all such cases, the Cabinet secretariat took the final call.

An important invitee to the Cabinet meetings was the deputy chairman of the Planning Commission. The Planning Commission was not a government department but an autonomous body under the Ministry of Planning. The PM was the chairman of the Planning Commission as well as the minister in charge of planning. The deputy chairman of the Planning Commission was invited on a permanent basis to the Cabinet. In this respect, he had a unique position. Montek Singh Ahluwalia, who was appointed by the UPA, was punctilious in attending meetings, and during discussions often put forth his views with great clarity.

Very often, ministers arrived much before the scheduled time for the meeting. I recall one such occasion, when, as I entered the Cabinet room, Arjun Singh remarked jocularly, 'We should adjust our watches, as when the Cabinet secretary arrives, the scheduled time for the meeting has struck.' It was clearly also a comment on me, as I invariably arrived for such meetings a few minutes early. I got the impression that being quite senior in the party, he was not very comfortable with the decision to have Dr Singh as the choice of PM. However, that was never the case with Pranab Mukherjee, also a very senior minister. He never gave me the impression of any resentment for not having been offered the post of PM by Mrs Gandhi.

Dr Singh expanded his Cabinet in 2006. The day the expansion was scheduled, early in the morning an official of the Cabinet secretariat came to my residence. For the Cabinet expansion planned, we were to inform the concerned ministers who were to be sworn in that day. While all the others had been informed, there was a problem with one name. The President had approved full Cabinet rank for M. Deora. Now this could have been either Murli Deora, the father, or Milind Deora, the son. We had informed Milind Deora, as Murli Deora was generally referred to by his full name. Murli Deora argued on the telephone that his name had been approved by the President and while he would be happy even if his son were appointed a minister, that was not the case here. He also mentioned that he had received the same information from his political network. I asked him to wait and checked on my part. And, indeed, it was Murli Deora whose name had been approved—but his name had been referred to in short form. He joined the Cabinet after taking oath that day.

After the expansion, the strength of the Cabinet increased to seventy-nine. In 2003, a Constitutional amendment* with several

---

*These amendments were made in the Constitution (Ninety-First Amendment) Act, 2003. The National Commission to Review the Working of the Constitution, or the NCRWC, had observed that abnormally large councils of ministers were being constituted by various governments at the Centre and at the states, and this practice had to be prohibited by law and a ceiling fixed on the number of ministers in a state or the Union government at a maximum of 10 per cent

salutary provisions had been passed by the Vajpayee government. While its main thrust was limiting the number of ministers in Central and state Cabinets to 15 per cent of the strength of the lower house, with a minimum of twelve ministers, it also further tightened the anti-defection law, with a minimum two-third majority required to split a party. The spirit of the Constitutional amendment was to improve political governance by keeping a ministry compact. However, in actual practice, the limit was invariably crossed. Even when parties promised to have 'minimum government and maximum governance', like the present Narendra Modi-led NDA, once in power, the number of ministers in the government very soon reached the ceiling permitted under the Constitution. The current NDA government had started with forty-five ministers in May 2014 but, within six months, increased to sixty-six and thereafter to seventy-eight in the next expansion. In matters of governance, the Union government has to act as a model for the states. Efforts to keep ministries small, however, have not happened.

During the course of my long years working in the government, I have found that a large number of the offices of state ministers are not really required. Many of them are usually without any substantive work. Also, many ministries need to be merged to improve performance and have better coordination. For example, as is the international practice, the Ministry of Road Transport and Highways needs to combine all modes of transport—road, rail, air and sea—and state ministers need to be in charge of each sector. In many international conferences, as a member of the Planning

---

of the total strength of the popular House of the Legislature. The government decided to fix this at 15 per cent.

Commission looking after transport, I represented the Government of India, as all other nations had a minister for transport looking after all modes. Similarly, the Ministry of Power must look after all modes—petroleum, power, coal and renewable energy—with state ministers supporting the work. There is a clear need to evolve new, healthy traditions to limit the number of ministers. We need to amend the Constitution once again to limit the size of ministries to not more than 12 per cent of the strength of the Lok Sabha (or, say, sixty-five ministers) or of the lower house of the states.

The Cabinet and the Super Cabinet

Decision-making by the Cabinet is a complex process. Once the Cabinet note is circulated for consideration, it is taken up for discussion. The note always specifies the points on which Cabinet approval is required. In the early years, the Cabinet secretary would initiate the discussion. The minister of the department concerned would add some details, and then the members of the Cabinet would express their views. Finally, the Cabinet would take a decision. The PM would mention this at the end of the discussion. Secretaries to the government would wait in the anteroom to provide any clarification, if required. The idea behind the entire system was to preserve the confidentiality of the Cabinet discussion. It also ensured that the concerned ministers were fully briefed on the issues going to the Cabinet.

Over the years, this has changed. The secretary of the concerned department is invariably called inside the Cabinet room and seated behind the ministers. The concerned minister intervenes in the discussion and then asks the secretary of the department to supplement it. The discussion is often led by the concerned secretary, and clarification, when called for by any Cabinet minister, is given by him. This has in the past caused some problems. There was an instance when, during the time I was petroleum secretary in the Vajpayee government, the Cabinet had to approve investment in an oil block in Africa. During the extensive discussion, the Petroleum Minister, Ram Naik, insisted that I respond to queries raised by Jaswant Singh, the external affairs minister then. Though he did not object to this practice on the first two instances, on the third occasion, Jaswant Singh commented that he could not possibly argue this with the secretary. The issue was postponed. But the message was clear—many ministers did not like discussions with secretaries. There was also the issue of confidentiality of Cabinet discussions.

When the new government under Dr Singh took over, for some time the existing process continued. I do not recall the trigger for change but within a few weeks of my taking over as Cabinet secretary, the PM decided that the older system would be revived. As a result, all items of the Cabinet started getting presented by me. While doing so, I also had to point out the opposition to the proposal, if any, and the response of the ministry sponsoring the proposal. The discussions would then be taken over by the ministers. After some time, the PM would call me to respond to the issues raised during the discussions and then approve the proposal or send it to a group of ministers or committee of secretaries. At times, the minister would request the presence of his secretary to explain a point. This was, however, rare.

The Cabinet meetings had several implications for me. The range of issues to be covered was wide and varied. It required a thorough understanding of the issues involved. Often, the proposals were opposed by other ministries. It then required an understanding of the reasons involved and whether the response of the ministry to the objection was justified and could be supported. While the PM gave directions on each proposal, at times he would ask for my advice on the future course of action. This required a thorough understanding of the issues involved.

In the initial period of the government, most of the issues would be decided by the Cabinet straightaway. At times, the PM would send the issues on which there was sharp disagreement for consideration by the committee of secretaries (CoS), which basically comprised secretaries of ministries concerned with the Cabinet proposal. If an issue had large political dimensions to be considered, it was referred to a group of ministers (GoM). In the CoS, I would let the matter be discussed and then take a view on merit, which was suitable administratively. Even if a secretary objected to a proposal, the decision was mine and I would at times overrule the concerned secretary to arrive at the best decision. The views of the ministry, which often reflected the views of the minister of the department, thus got overruled or modified in the CoS decision, which would then go to the Cabinet and invariably get approved. The ministers did not like it.

Gradually, the ministers started suggesting the formation of a GoM when there were differences in the Cabinet and no decision was arrived at. This was usually chaired by the minister of the concerned department that had sent the proposal to the Cabinet. This provided a clear edge to them as against the CoS, which was chaired by the Cabinet secretary. With coalition pressures getting stronger, the GoM became a more popular mode of decision-making in the event of difference of views among the departments.

When issues were referred by the Cabinet for the GoM's views, unlike the CoS, the ministers of the Group invariably had a political input in decision-making. Quite often, the meetings would get delayed as the ministers had other commitments. Further, if the Cabinet meeting was not scheduled in a certain week, the decisions got even more delayed. As the number of issues coming to the Cabinet increased, many differences of opinion in departments started getting referred to the GoMs. With negative comments from several ministries, the matter was referred to the GoMs led by senior ministers. Pranab Mukherjee was the next senior minister to the PM, and many GoMs were constituted under his chairmanship. He had a wide experience of different ministries and understood complex governance issues well. Also, coalition partners knew that he was in the best position to overrule (this was rare) any Congress minister who was being unreasonable in their stand in the Cabinet.

With the constitution of GoMs, an easy way was found to consider issues that had no unanimity among ministries. The number of GoMs started proliferating. There were more than fifty GoMs with Pranab Mukherjee. This, in a way, transferred the decision-making power of the Cabinet to the GoM, since invariably the decision of the GoMs was approved by the Cabinet without further discussion.

The problem with the GoM system of decision-making in the coalition Cabinet was that there were too many of them. As a result, the GoM at times referred the issue to a committee of officials or to another committee chaired by a member of the Planning Commission. The GoM, though an excellent institutional device, was used much too often. This delayed decision-making and reduced its effectiveness as an instrument of governance.

The decision by GoMs had another dimension. If there was no unanimity on an issue, an area that everyone agreed to was taken as the decision. This was particularly harmful where vital policy issues were involved. I recall the problem of coal for power plants. There were objections from the Ministry of Environment & Forests (MoEF). In spite of an extensive report on the issue with the GoM, which dealt with the prevailing problems of availability of coal in the power, steel and cement sector and suggested a way to sort them out, the view of the ministry prevailed, with some dilutions suggested by it. The coal availability continued to be poor. This resulted in a shortage of domestic coal for the steel and cement industry, and huge delays in the commissioning of power plants. Given the large investment in the power sector, this decision subsequently led to stranded power-sector assets and non-performing assets (NPAs) of banks.

But Cabinet meetings had interesting sidelights too. After I would present an item and it had been placed for consideration by the Cabinet, a number of ministers would put forth their points of view. Two members always argued their cases cogently— P. Chidambaram and Montek Singh Ahluwalia. In fact, I recall how forcefully Chidambaram argued for the creation of posts and the appointment of a large number of officials in the Finance Ministry, which he headed. The official policy was to curb the creation of any such post. Every minister was opposed to the Finance Ministry's proposal. But Chidambaram argued that the new posts were meant to plug leakage of taxes, as the number of income tax payers was increasing and there was a lack of adequate scrutiny. Later, it was approved by the Cabinet.

I would at times get informal notes from members while a discussion was going on in the Cabinet. Such notes were written on a small chit, folded and passed to me via a Cabinet secretariat official. These were on widely different issues—requests for quickly filling up some vacancies in the ministry or in their personal staff or other posts; suggestions for action on certain issues, especially price rise; requests for taking up a Cabinet item early; or a plea for addressing injustice done to some officer.

While the Cabinet meetings were generally smooth affairs, on one particular occasion it caused me a lot of embarrassment due to a communication gap with the PMO. This meeting was about passing a condolence resolution. Such meetings were called at very short notice and had a one-point agenda—to condole the death of some eminent person. The Cabinet in these cases considered and passed a resolution to convey the government's decision to share their grief with the family of the deceased. These resolutions also included details of the services rendered to the nation by the departed leader or official, which was prepared by the Cabinet secretariat based on material available from the Parliament's website or other credible sources. At times, when these resolutions were being considered by the Cabinet, ministers suggested changes to incorporate a more detailed description. On one such occasion, K. Natwar Singh, who was a Cabinet minister, offered to elaborate on it and describe the services of the departed leader—and this was agreed to. On one such occasion, adequate copies of the condolence resolution (updated and modified) were put on the table and a copy was given to the staff of the PM. Unfortunately, the modified version of the condolence resolution did not reach the PM. So when I started reading the Cabinet resolution in the meeting, as was the practice, all ministers had this modified version, except the PM. This was a faux pas. We never talked about it later.

I recall another meeting of the Cabinet, in which Dayanidhi Maran proposed a policy for investment in the telecom sector, which Chidambaram opposed. The two ministers from Tamil Nadu had an uneasy relationship. The PM asked me to look into it. When I consulted the principal secretary, he suggested that there was a solution on which both ministers could agree. I did not find this halfway house acceptable and wanted to look at it on the basis of merit. So I called a meeting of experts and sought their views. I also consulted Ratan Tata, Ashok Ganguly and Deepak Parekh, who were members of the investment commission in the Ministry of Finance. When I placed the recommendations before the Cabinet, both Chidambaram and Maran agreed to it, but both wanted one or two amendments to the proposal. The amendments desired by one differed from the other's. The PM ruled that either they had to accept the whole proposal or he would send the matter for further consideration by a GoM. Both ministers promptly agreed to the recommendations thereafter.

Over a period of three years, I must have dealt with several hundred Cabinet notes. By their very nature, these dealt with important policy issues. I want to select two instances for analysis here. While doing this, I will comment on how certain important policy issues were considered by the Cabinet. This will also indicate how certain decisions had little administrative input, and others, in spite of having been referred to a GoM, were decided through the intervention of civil servants.

Delhi and Mumbai Airports

The process of decision-making often raises important issues of governance, as illustrated in the case of the selection of a private developer as a joint venture (JV) partner for the modernization of the Delhi and Mumbai airports.* At that time, the Airports Authority of India (AAI), an organization under the Ministry of Civil Aviation, had invited bids for selecting such a partner. It was a two-stage process. In the first stage, the bidders had to be selected based on technical qualification. For this, marks were awarded for each prescribed parameter. The marks for technical qualification were fairly high. Also, the financial bid was opened only to those bidders who had qualified technically. In this case, a technical consultant, and later a group of officials under the chairmanship of the secretary of civil aviation, had assessed the bids and awarded marks to each bidder. The Planning Commission representative felt that the assessment had not been done in accordance with the norms of the request for proposal (RFP) and should not be accepted. The Cabinet had earlier formed a GoM to look at this entire process of modernization. They were in a fix, as assessment of bids was a technical matter, and there should not have been differences among the officials. They decided to send the issue to a CoS under me for advice.

All such projects invariably see the participation of powerful industrial groups. This was no exception. In the first CoS meeting,

---

*The facts on this have been taken primarily from the judgement of the Supreme Court on 7 November 2006, delivered by Justice Arijit Pasayat in the appeal filed by Reliance Developers with the Airports Authority of India and others as respondent. Accessed 23 February 2019, https://indiankanoon.org/doc/379361/

it was suggested by the Ministry of Civil Aviation that since the committee that I chaired had a number of secretaries, each of them should look at one bidder, along with the assessment of marks awarded to it. I was confirmed in my belief that secretaries to the government were not experts in tender evaluation and credible professional advice was needed. After some discussion, it was decided to appoint a committee under E. Sreedharan, who had built the Konkan Railway and the Delhi Metro, to look at the entire tendering process and produce a report. Sreedharan had an impeccable record for honesty and uprightness, and his report would carry great credibility. He was to be assisted by a former financial advisor of the Railways, who, too, had an impeccable record. This group was later referred to as the Group of Eminent Technical Experts (GETE). In about a week, his report was with us and was approved by the CoS. He clearly identified only one bidder as having technically qualified the bidding process. The GoM decided to accept the recommendations and proceed accordingly.

I was sure that this issue would now go to court. It was, therefore, important that all facts were available in one document. I called the joint secretary of the civil aviation ministry and asked him to prepare a note that highlighted the entire process, including Sreedharan's appointment. The ministry was initially hesitant but finally agreed to this approach. Later, as these issues were agitated in courts, the facts were placed before them and the GETE decision/report was upheld by the SC. The case, however, raised certain important issues of governance:

- The selection process of the JV partner took a lot of time and, in spite of engaging eminent international firms for bid evaluation, the process was initially not fair. It would have gone through but for an objection by a representative of the Planning Commission. It took GETE to make a final correct evaluation. So any large-scale development of infrastructure needs simpler procedures.

- When any such JV is formed, initially there are terms of the project implementation, including transfer of land, sharing of revenue and project completion. If there is an overrun or the scope of the project is subsequently enhanced, new terms may have to be added to the agreed conditions. This may amount to providing extra benefits to the private partner and hence invite criticism. How do we handle these project needs?
- The selection of the company as the JV partner can only be the first step. There are other agreements required—including the state support agreement (SSA), the operation, maintenance and development agreement (OMDA), the shareholders' agreement (SHA) and the lease deed agreement, among others. These provisions can be interpreted by the government and the auditors differently. Government officials involved in this may later be accused of having given undue benefits to the JV company. It can put any further process of modernization on hold and slow down decision-making.

President's Rule in Bihar: Where We Erred

While Cabinet decisions are invariably arrived at after a great deal of consultation, there are certain issues that are, by their very nature, affected by the political complexion of the party ruling at the Centre. Of these, one of the areas that is always discussed extensively in the public domain is the use of Article 356 of the Constitution (which carries the marginal heading 'Provisions in Case of Failure of Constitutional Machinery in States'). During my tenure, the Cabinet considered the decision to impose President's rule in Bihar* after elections were held in the state for constitution of the State Legislative Assembly in February 2005. The elections did not throw up a clear mandate in favour of any political party or an alliance of parties formed prior to the election process. It also did not indicate any coalition at that time which could lay claim to a majority and the running of the government. There were two groups, both of which could not reach the halfway mark of 122 MLAs. Considering this position, the governor of Bihar, Buta Singh, sent a recommendation mentioning various facts and suggested the imposition of President's rule and keeping the Assembly in suspended animation, as the term of the earlier Assembly was expiring in early March. This was approved by the Union Cabinet and a notification imposing President's rule on the state was issued on 7 March. This was nothing unusual and did not attract any criticism. The intention, clearly, was to use the next few months to enable the normal political process to take over and give time to various political leaders to muster a coalition that had a majority. This sentiment was expressed by Home Minister Shivraj Patil, while speaking in the Parliament.

Despite the noble intentions of the government, there were

---

*The Bihar Assembly Dissolution Case in 2005, accessed 23 February 2018
http://www.ebc-india.com/downloads/bihar_Assembly_dissolution_case_1.pdf

undercurrents of unease in Delhi as the RJD, which was a major alliance partner of the UPA, could see that things were not moving in its favour. The RJD, which had won seventy-five seats, was still far from the halfway mark, which would give it the right to form the government. The events were moving towards a majority for Janata Dal (United), or JD(U), supported by the Bharatiya Janata Party (BJP), and getting support of Lok Jan Shakti (LJP) party.

The governor sent reports on 27 April, and finally on 22 May. He apprised the government of the developments in Bihar's political scene on government formation after the elections, and mentioned that various allurements of money, caste and post were being offered to MLAs. The JD(U) was targeting the LJP and its sixteen or seventeen MLAs, which were being won over by them; and they wanted to form the government with the support of the BJP. The governor mentioned reports that the JD(U) was planning a split in the Congress too. He found this disturbing and against the provisions of the Constitution, that a majority was being cobbled in this corrupt manner. His argument was that in the interest of democracy, a majority should not be stitched together by horse-trading or other questionable means. He referred to the report of the National Commission to Review the Working of the Constitution (NCRWC), which had termed unprincipled and opportunistic political alliance as a mockery of democracy. In view of the above, he recommended the dissolution of the Bihar Assembly in his final report.

I recall the agitation among RJD ministers and others when the Cabinet met. It was often mentioned during informal discussions that to cobble a majority in the Bihar Assembly, a lot of unfair means, including the use of money, was being resorted to. Later, when the home ministry put forward a proposal for the dissolution of the Assembly, the members of the Cabinet were excited. I noticed among them a feeling that justice was being done and that the nefarious machinations of somehow developing a majority in the Assembly and grabbing power were being defeated.

On the day the approval of the dissolution of the Bihar Assembly was taken by the Cabinet, the meeting was slated after dinner. It was rather late, as the Ministry of Home Affairs (MHA) was taking time to finalize its Cabinet note. So when we assembled for the Cabinet meeting, the note was still not with us. A number of excited Cabinet ministers were of the view that the note could be taken on record as it was getting delayed, and the proposal could be approved. Finally, when the note was circulated, the Cabinet did not take much time to approve it. Members had already made up their minds. I do not recall a single dissenting voice at that time. The rest of the process, including finalizing the Cabinet minutes, was completed quickly. The proposal now required the approval of the President. But A.P.J. Abdul Kalam was out of the country. A message containing the proposal was sent to him. After his approval, a notification was issued and the Assembly was dissolved.

The dissolution was severely criticized by the SC and the propriety of President Kalam agreeing to it was also questioned. The court, in its judgement, which was a split decision, held:

> If a political party with the support of other political party or other MLAs stakes claim to form a Government and satisfies the Governor about its majority to form a stable Government, the Governor cannot refuse formation of Government and

override the majority claim because of his subjective assessment that the majority was cobbled by illegal and unethical means. No such power has been vested with the Governor. Such a power would be against the democratic principles of majority rule. Governor is not an autocratic political Ombudsman. If such a power is vested in the Governor and/or the President, the consequences can be horrendous. The ground of mal-administration by a State Government enjoying majority is not available for invoking power under Article 356. The remedy for corruption or similar ills and evils lies elsewhere and not in Article 356(1).*

I must confess that with all the reports sent by the governor of money playing a part in cobbling a majority, I saw ethical values having very low priority in the formation of a government. This case raised several questions that are important for our governance.

How do we ensure that the post-election realignment in any Assembly is not because of money paid to legislators supporting the new group laying claim to form the government? Should we assume that, despite the level of corruption prevailing in our polity, all independent members are giving support to a government because they don't want another round of election? Should the governor not be concerned with how the majority has been cobbled? How do we ensure that post-election results and a hung Assembly, or a 'change of heart' of lawmakers does not take place because of money being offered? How do we disregard the fact that there is massive corruption in our polity and many politicians will do

---

*Case No.: Writ Petition (Civil) 257 of 2005, accessed 17 March 2019
https://www.sci.gov.in/jonew/judis/27435.pdf

anything to be part of the government? Should winning a trust vote in the legislature be the ultimate test, irrespective of how it is arrived at? In short, how can ethical values and principles be more strongly woven into our democracy? There are no answers to these questions in the current functioning of the system.

It is equally important to reflect on the conduct of many governors and the Central government, which has not always been above board when no party had a majority after the elections. The governors are the appointees of the Central government, which advises the President. Many of them are former politicians and maintain their links with political parties in power. There are some former officials who are also governors of states and, in most cases, may be happy to do the bidding of the Central government. So in situations where no party has had a majority after elections to a State Assembly, the Central government has often tended to misuse its power to gain political advantage. The devolution of powers to the Centre and the functioning of State Legislatures had come in for extensive discussion in the constituent Assembly. Dr B.R. Ambedkar had hoped that this provision would be used very rarely and remain 'a dead letter'.*

---

*'In regard to the general debate which has taken place, in which it has been suggested that these articles are liable to be abused, I may say that I do not altogether deny that there is a possibility of these articles being abused or employed for political purposes. But that objection applies to every part of the Constitution which gives power to the Centre to override the provinces. In fact, I share the sentiments expressed by my honourable friend Mr Gupte that the proper thing we ought to expect is that such articles will never be called into operation and that they would remain a dead letter. If at all they are brought into operation, I hope the President, who is endowed with these powers, will take proper precautions before actually suspending the administration of the provinces.'

Our founding fathers felt that if in certain states the government could not be carried on in accordance with the Constitution, the President must initially warn them that they were not carrying on as per Constitutional provision. This was expected to set things right. If all this failed, the imposition of President's rule was to be considered. Unfortunately, the article has become a tool in the hands of the government at the Centre for destabilizing political parties of different complexion. It has been misused to further the political interest of the party at the Centre.

Unique Governance Model: Clear Division of Power

A unique feature of UPA-I was the setting up of the NAC, an important institution presided over by Mrs Gandhi. The twelve-member council, which included former senior civil servants, economists, health and education experts, food security experts and activists working in non-governmental organizations (NGOs), was to act as a think tank and advise the government on a range of policy issues. This institution provided a lot of ideas to the government for policy. Since it was chaired by Mrs Gandhi, who had declined to be named PM but clearly had full control of the Party, it emerged as a strong centre of power even on policy matters.

I had no direct interaction with the deliberations of the NAC. In 2013, however, I was asked to make a presentation to the NAC on the development in the Northeast region and also brief them on the implementation of some of the suggestions made earlier

Constituent Assembly Debates on 4 August 1949 Part I, accessed 16 March 2019 https://indiankanoon.org/doc/1333892/

by the committee on the issue. In my presentation, I gave details of accelerated focus by the Planning Commission on the region and the expansion of the air, rail and road network. Mrs Gandhi listened with interest but remained quiet during the discussions that followed. Later, I learnt from some members that she always allowed discussion to proceed on most subjects so that members could have their say. Clearly, she was a good listener.

The functioning of the NAC was reflective of a policymaking institution with a different approach. The NAC was strongly influenced by the rights approach, which, at times, did not fully consider financial or administrative implications. It had a strong influence of the NGO sector. Many of its proposals looked at the benefits to be provided to tribals, women and minorities. This gave it the image of a pro-poor institution. There was continuous interaction between the NAC and the government to ensure their proposals reflected the ground realities too. When the NAC sent suggestions, these were looked at carefully by us in the CoS. There was no pressure to accept it, but departments were clearly conscious of the fact that the proposal had the backing of the NAC.

Several NAC proposals were forward-looking. The Right to Information (RTI) Act, for example, was sent by the NAC after extensive discussion. This was a key initiative, which focused on transparency in administration. The government initially had reservations about several of its provisions, and these were diluted. When these went to the Parliamentary Committee, several of these were restored to their original positions. Clearly, the political power backed the NAC position. The government, too, then accepted the changes. Given the need to provide employment in rural areas, the passing of the Mahatma Gandhi National Rural Employment

Guarantee Act (MGNREGA) 2005 was another important initiative by them. The amendment to the Hindu Succession Act, 1956, to enable daughters to have a share in the ancestral property of their father, was yet another progressive step suggested by it.

Often, the departments would make presentations before the NAC to sort out issues before policy proposals were implemented. There was extensive discussion, for example between the government and the NAC, on parameters of certain policies such as the National Food Security Act, 2013. The basic limitation was the availability of food with the government procurement agency and the extent of the subsidy burden. The NAC wanted a high availability and cheaper food. The government clearly had limitations, as the procurement was of certain limited quantities only, and it did not wish to make the subsidy burden very high. The final Bill which was passed in the Parliament was a realistic law based on the marriage of the two positions.

But there were certain other NAC proposals that were unrealistic. I recall that one such proposal was the draft of a law to provide better protection to minorities, which was completely unworkable. There were other proposals from the NAC, such as the Bill for changes in the Land Acquisition Act, 2013, which were supported by a large body of public representatives and MPs but had administrative problems. The Bill was passed as an Act of Parliament and called the Right to Fair Compensation and Transparency in Land Acquisition, Rehabilitation and Resettlement Act, 2013. This Act has caused serious problems in getting land quickly for developing infrastructure and industries, and the states have had to work out various methods to get around it.

The system of governance devised at that time had a clear

division of power. While Dr Singh was responsible for running the administration of the country as the PM, Mrs Gandhi wielded political power. She, however, was part of the core group, presided over by the PM, which included a few ministers apart from Ahmed Patel, who was an MP and political secretary to Mrs Gandhi. The group met every week at the residence of the PM to discuss various issues. The NAC gave some excellent ideas and helped with policymaking, which was mostly inclined towards greater support for the weaker sections of society. Its very presence, however, gave the impression of an alternative centre of political power that was running the show. This did not give good media presence for the government.

As an institution of governance, this arrangement devised by the UPA had some major advantages. As a distinguished civil servant, Dr Singh had excellent ideas about the system of governance prevailing in our country. He had been part of the Congress since he had decided to enter politics and, unlike many other leaders, had never shifted his loyalty to any other formation or political group. He had practically no political base of his own and was likely to be loyal to the Party. Also, he was simple in his living style and had an impeccable reputation for honesty and uprightness. On the other hand, Mrs Gandhi had no experience at all of running either the government at the Centre or at the states. Her strength was an excellent background in running the Party. So the arrangement seemed perfect, with the two of them functioning in their respective areas of specialization, and coordination provided by the core group.

This experiment, however, had problems that could not be seen clearly in 2004. The PMO has both political and administrative dimensions. The PM participates in parliamentary proceedings, interacts with political leaders of different parties and keeps watch on the performance of ministers. Dr Singh was extremely bright but not an orator. His parliamentary speeches often reflected this position. A lot of floor management was required in the Lok Sabha, as coalition partners often had their own positions on certain issues. There was also need for close political interface with the Opposition parties. But the most important part of the limitation of this arrangement was that ministers tended to look to Mrs Gandhi rather than only to the PM. While they were respectful of the PM, it was clear that as ministers, they owed their positions as much, if not more, to Mrs Gandhi. With respect to coalition partners, the Congress president had a major say, as she had stitched the arrangement together. Ministers of coalition partners were nominees of those parties. The PM had to manage them even when he was not happy with a nominee. While she gave full respect to the PM and the meetings of the core group were invariably held at 7 Race Course Road, the PM's residence, there was no doubt that she was a strong power centre. All this was not helpful in improving the overall functioning of the government. I would like to quote two instances that amplify this point.

Sanjaya Baru had been media advisor to the PM earlier and had later moved to Singapore on another assignment. When the UPA won the elections in 2009, there was a proposal to reappoint him as the media advisor. He was apparently given this indication during his informal interaction with Dr Singh. Baru had worked closely with him, was well qualified and extremely experienced. He left his job in Singapore and moved to Delhi, preparing himself for his new job. But this appointment did not materialize. While it is difficult to say what happened, it appeared that for some reason,

Baru was not acceptable to the Party and the proposal, therefore, did not fructify.

The second instance relates to the approval of an ordinance by the Cabinet to provide protection to convicted MPs and MLAs, in September 2013. The intention of the proposed law was that if an appeal was pending, politicians convicted of a crime could not be debarred from contesting elections. It was felt that this was aimed at providing protection to Lalu Prasad Yadav in the fodder scam case. During the course of a press conference in Delhi, Rahul Gandhi, who was the vice president of the Party at that time, showed strong resentment against this policy and tore the copy of the ordinance. This was a strong public indictment of the government from within, and did not reflect well on it.

Yet another fallout of this special arrangement was that when attacks were mounted on the PM as corruption charges were made against the government, there was very little coordinated effort by the Congress, the UPA ministers or other politicians to strongly put forward the government's viewpoint, speak up in his favour and strongly defend him. When I contrast this position with the current NDA government, where any criticism is met vehemently by ministers and through social media, the difference is stark. This position did not give the impression of a government that was fully united. It adversely affected its public image.

Dealing with Political Instability

Pulls and pressures are part of a coalition, and any occasion can be used to display the inherent instability of such a structure. The first destabilizing factor proved to be K. Chandrasekhar Rao (KCR), president of the Telangana Rashtra Samithi (TRS), who had been sworn in as Cabinet minister of Labour and Employment. His Party was a constituent of the UPA. During my interaction with him, I got an impression that he was uncomfortable for some reason. He did not last long and resigned from the Cabinet. With KCR's exit, the TRS withdrew its support to the government and its lone state minister resigned. While the moving away of the TRS as a coalition partner was not significant in terms of numbers, major partners such as the DMK were crucial to the stability of the government. This was evident when, on the occasion of a scheduled Cabinet meeting, the PM, who generally arrived within minutes of the scheduled time, was unduly delayed. There was no indication of when the PM would arrive. I noticed that several ministers of the DMK were absent, which was rather strange. The South Block Cabinet room, where the meeting was scheduled, was only a couple of rooms away from the PM's office. We were informed that the DMK ministers were meeting the PM and that he would arrive shortly. After a few minutes, the DMK ministers came to the Cabinet room and the PM arrived a little later. It was apparent that these ministers had gone to convey the message that they wanted greater accommodation in the running of the government.

That coalitions are, at times, threatened by unforeseen events was evident in October 2005, when a strong and loyal supporter of the Congress party had to leave the Cabinet. Natwar Singh was considered close to Mrs Gandhi and had also worked very closely with Rajiv Gandhi earlier. He was initially moved out as the minister for external affairs and made minister without portfolio as a result of a report by Paul A. Volcker. Volcker was a former chairman of the US Federal Reserve Bank who had been appointed by the

United Nations (UN) Secretary General to inquire into allegations of misuse of the oil-for-food programme started by the UN to meet the requirement of foodgrains in Iraq when the regime of Saddam Hussein, its former president, was in power. There were complaints that the oil ministry of Iraq was giving oil vouchers, which were being used by middlemen to earn money.

Volcker's report, which was released on 27 October 2005, contained a list of persons who were beneficiaries of these oil permits given by the Saddam regime. The list mentioned the Congress party and Jagat Singh, Natwar Singh's son, as non-contractual beneficiaries. It was later alleged that during a visit of a Congress party delegation to Baghdad, Jagat had used his father's influence on the Saddam regime to get permission for selling oil.

Several countries started their own inquiries to ascertain whether their officials or other citizens had committed any wrong in circumventing and misusing the UN sanctions. We also started our own inquiries into the matter through the Enforcement Directorate (ED) to ascertain whether our laws had been violated. Later, the matter was entrusted to a former chief justice of India, R.S. Pathak, who initiated an independent inquiry into the entire matter. Efforts were made to get all relevant documents from New York and Baghdad. Natwar Singh was shifted from the Ministry of Foreign Affairs in less than a fortnight of the receipt of the Volcker report. He became a minister without portfolio in November, when the appointment of the Justice Pathak Commission was announced. However, within a month, Natwar Singh resigned as minister. The enquiry conducted by Justice Pathak finally produced its report in August 2006 and did not find Natwar Singh and his son guilty of any financial transaction or wrongdoing, but indicted them for getting three contracts for oil using their influence which were subsequently misused by two persons, Andaleeb Sehgal and Aditya Khanna, to get commissions by selling the allocation to a Swiss company. He did not find the Congress party a contractual beneficiary.

The impact of the weakness inherent in the coalition structure came to the fore when Dr Singh decided to strike a nuclear deal in July 2005 with the George W. Bush administration of the US. This was considered a major development in Indo-US relations and India being recognized as a nuclear power by the global community. The deal was hailed in India as a major breakthrough for improving energy security. A lot of groundwork for strengthening relations with the US had earlier been done by Brajesh Mishra.

After the PM's return from his US visit in July 2005, as I finished my briefing, I asked him how he was able to achieve the breakthrough on the difficult question of the US's recognizing India as a state with nuclear-power capabilities.

In his usual quiet manner, Dr Singh said that after the 1974 explosion of India's nuclear device and subsequent action by many countries, including the US, people in India did not feel emotionally close to the people of the US. By recognizing India's nuclear status and giving it access to modern cutting-edge sensitive technologies, this perception in India could change dramatically. He insisted that this opportunity could not be missed.

After the PM's talk with the US, things changed dramatically between India and the US, leading to a more positive approach to India's being armed with nuclear power.

The Left parties were, however, unhappy with the government for maintaining close relations with the US and further developing it with the nuclear deal. It took three years for them to finally withdraw their support. On 9 July 2008, they issued a detailed statement outlining their reasons. It was mentioned that the strategic alliance with the US was not part of the CMP and that the deal would not provide energy security to India. They argued that provisions of the Hyde Amendment, a US-government legislation, would restrict implementation of the deal and not safeguard India's interests. They also objected to the government's decision to go ahead with the 123 Agreement with the US as part of the process to operationalize the nuclear deal, and continuing negotiations with the International Atomic Energy Agency (IAEA) on its safeguard agreement where our civil nuclear facilities were being identified.

They also argued that the Congress leadership had violated the understanding arrived at with the Left parties in November 2007, wherein the outcome of the talks with the secretariat of the IAEA was to be presented to the UPA-Left committee on the nuclear deal. Also, the PM had gone to the G8 summit in Japan and, before meeting President Bush, had announced that the government would be going to the IAEA board very soon. The Left parties hadn't known about this development. The Left also accused the UPA government of going back on its commitment of following an independent foreign policy, in contrast to the pro-American stand of the BJP-led government.

With the withdrawal of Left support, the majority of the coalition was in question. The trust vote took place in the Parliament on 22 July 2008, within a fortnight of the withdrawal. The government should have fallen, but it didn't. It was managed with help from Amar Singh and Mulayam Singh Yadav, general secretary and president of the SP, respectively. Efforts were made by Congress leaders to get support from other parties too, with their personal contacts. Also, independent and smaller political formations were approached, resulting in a lot of cross-voting. Former President Kalam also came out in favour of the nuclear deal, and many other scientists supported it. It was a murky affair. There were allegations of money being paid to MPs to get their support for the trust motion. A sting operation was conducted by a leading news channel to prove that this had indeed been happening. A bundle of notes was produced in the Parliament to prove that money was being offered to MPs in large quantities to save the government. During the trust vote, a number of MPs abstained. There was also cross-voting, in which the government lost some votes as a number of SP MPs were opposed to the nuclear deal. The list of people who voted for the trust resolution included several MPs who had earlier been fence sitters and not part of the UPA. The final tally of votes in favour of the government was 275, as opposed to the 256 against it.

In view of the allegations made during the proceedings, the charges of corruption were taken up for inquiry against two MPs, Ahmad Patel and Amar Singh, who were alleged to have been involved. The Joint Parliamentary Committee (JPC) did not find any evidence of bribe but suggested further investigation. The police registered a case, and Amar Singh, his aide, two BJP MPs and Sudheendra Kulkarni (who had allegedly masterminded the sting done by the TV channel) were arrested. Five years later, the court discharged all the accused, except Amar Singh's aide. It held that they had 'the intention to expose horse-trading', which was corroborated by the fact that currency notes were taken to the Parliament House and tabled to be viewed by the entire nation. The case, once again, raised issues regarding the role of money power in the functioning of the Parliament. Given the independence of the legislatures, how does one ensure probity when the casting of votes cannot be questioned even when money is offered for it? It is only events outside the house that the police investigates. There is need for a law under which such cases are investigated by an internal investigating team of the Parliament. If it finds prima facie evidence, the case should then be handed over to the police for regular investigation, and the legislature may waive its privilege in such cases.

Chapter 4

DUTY AND MATTERS OF CONSCIENCE

The process of governance gradually threw up a variety of issues. The problems of poor health services and low nutrition raised the question of high infant and maternal mortality rates in our country. The issues of unemployment and underemployment were already quite well known. The development of infrastructure had been inadequate so far and hindered the growth process. The per capita income was low, with lack of many basic amenities, such as education and energy, to a large number of people. The delivery of public services was inefficient and there was massive corruption in the system. Our systems and procedures were also not people-friendly. I looked at many of these aspects to improve our governance system.

I kept the PM briefed on the development of many of these governance issues in my periodic meetings with him. However, a separate arrangement was in place when the PM was abroad. The governance process proceeded as usual during this period. If, however, an urgent decision was required, generally one of the

Cabinet committees would meet (usually the Cabinet committee on political affairs) and take a decision on the further course of action. Considering the excellent communication facilities, need for such occasions arose rarely. During the foreign visits of the PM, we would send him a brief on major events and developments every day. Once or twice I would talk to him personally and brief him on the situation here. On one such occasion, I asked him how things were and how his visit was going, and Dr Singh gave a very interesting reply. He said, 'Chaturvedi, our major problems are in the country. Outside we are doing fine.' He was perhaps referring to India's success in handling foreign relations but its inadequate pace of change in the domestic economy.

There was an awkward moment for me during the PM's first visit to the US. While he had been with the government for nearly five decades, he was still a quiet person and did not believe in self-promotion. Very few people outside his family circle were, therefore, aware of his actual date of birth. I, unfortunately, had no idea about it. So when I rang up New York to brief the PM on the day's important events, his private secretary B.V.R. Subrahmanyam (or Subbu, as he was called), before passing on the phone to the PM, mentioned that it happened to be his birthday. I had clearly missed a common courtesy. So I thanked Subbu and wished Dr Singh on his first birthday after becoming PM. He was gracious as ever in his reply.

Iron Fist in a Velvet Glove

In the '60s and the '70s, law and order was primarily a state subject and handled by them. The only exception I recall where

Central intervention was needed was the Naxalite movement. But things have changed over the past three decades. Public-order problems have gradually become crucial at the national level, with terrorist activity expanding in many parts of the world. With organizations like Lashkar-e-Taiba (LeT), Jaish-e-Mohammad (JeM) and the Taliban active in Jammu and Kashmir (J&K), the threat from terrorism has increased. Separately, Left-wing extremism has gradually engulfed more than eighty districts in different states, with Chhattisgarh being one of the worst affected. The Northeast has problems of severe insurgency. All this has led to greater involvement of the Central government in law and order.

This was one of the issues I looked at closely. During my tenure as Cabinet secretary, there were a number of incidents in which there was a heavy loss of lives. Assam had been plagued by insurgency for a long time. A number of schoolchildren died in a bomb blast during the Independence Day celebration in 2004.

Over the next three years, there were more than half a dozen terrorist-related incidents in the country, in which about 400 people died. Of these, three stand out in my mind—the Mumbai train blast of 11 July 2006, the Diwali bomb blast of October 2005 in New Delhi's Sarojini Nagar and the Paharganj shopping area, and the blast in the Samjhauta Express heading for Pakistan in February 2007. There was terrorist activity in Varanasi, Malegaon and Hyderabad. Nearly seventy people died in these incidents. There was extensive left-wing-extremism (LWE) activity, which led to a huge loss of human life. The level of insurgent violence was high too. This, however, gradually decreased due to effective engagement with the leadership in different states and a strong focus on development. The MHA provided support to the states in the form of paramilitary forces and intelligence from IB and other sources. I had a fair idea of these developments and, in my meetings with the states, promoted the development of specially trained forces for handling hardcore Naxals.

J&K has been a major area of concern with all governments. The People's Democratic Party (PDP), supported by the Congress under a power-sharing arrangement, was in power in J&K since 2002, with Mufti Mohammad Sayeed as the CM. The state had seen a lot of terrorist activity in the past two decades. The fatalities were more than 5,000, including about 3,000 terrorists. There were clear signs of a thaw in our relationship with Pakistan during the PDP regime. Terrorist activity, however, continued but on a lower scale. In September 2004, the PM announced a financial package of ₹24,000 crore for the development of J&K. Mufti Sahib's term as CM was to end in 2005, with the Congress nominee to take over for the next three years. It appeared that Ghulam Nabi Azad was keen that the arrangement, under which the Congress and the PDP were to share power for three years each, be implemented. The PM, I got an impression, had reservations, as the PDP government was doing fine. Finally, a political decision was taken. In 2005, Ghulam Nabi took over as CM. The period saw a gradual decline in terrorist violence in Kashmir. India and Pakistan agreed on several measures to strengthen contacts between people of the two countries, specifically between J&K and Pakistan-occupied Kashmir (PoK). This led to the start of the Srinagar–Muzaffarabad bus service, the Samjhauta Express between Delhi and Lahore and a rail service connecting Rajasthan and Sindh. Trade relations at the border also strengthened. The period saw a sharp rise in Amarnath yatris. Nearly 3–4 lakh pilgrims would visit the shrine every year during this period.

Generally, I kept myself abreast of these developments, with inputs from IB, the J&K government, the home secretary and the concerned ministries. At times, there would be discussions and presentations by the National Security Council Secretariat. During my meetings with the PM, I would often brief him on various developments.

Developmental Initiatives

Considering the massive need for development of the basic necessities and for people to have an improved quality of life, several initiatives were being taken by the government. Rather early in my term, the PM asked me to resolve differences between Commerce Minister Kamal Nath and Finance Minister Chidambaram. The issue was the EXIM, or export import, policy of the government, which was important for stimulating exports, to be announced in a few days. It was a huge task, as there were more than 200 items, and the two ministers had serious differences. I called the two secretaries. Having worked in both ministries, I had a fair idea of the approach of both. After a detailed discussion, the recommendations were made. The Finance Minister rang me up and expressed his unhappiness with my findings on some items. But the policy was finalized in terms of my decision in the CoS. While economic policies and programmes were being made by the government to sharply reduce poverty and accelerate economic growth, there was a clear realization that access to health and education was basic to every person. There were programmes such as the National Rural Health Mission (NRHM), the RTI Act and the National Rural Employment Guarantee Act (now MGNREGA). Several of these made major contributions to improving governance. I intervened in many cases to improve the processes and make them people-friendly. There were other areas that required investments, or even new programmes. Invariably, these were also discussed in the CoS for resolving interministerial differences. Such occasions also gave me a good idea of the nature of the new initiatives.

The concept of access to electricity being integral to villagers' basic needs was not yet prevalent. This was taken up sometime in 2006. In those days, electrification of villages was in miserable shape. The position of electrification of rural households was worse. The Ministry of Power had a definition of electrification of villages which practically considered a village electrified even if a power line passed through it. Also, the number of people in the country with access to electricity* was merely 55 per cent. Thus, half the population did not have access to electricity for their domestic use. A proposal was brought at that time by the Ministry of Power to the CoS to modify the definition of village electrification, along with a plan to provide electricity to all households in the country. The financial provision for this was also indicated. There was strong opposition from the Planning Commission to this. They observed that the provision was highly understated and that the actual expenditure would be several times more. We discussed this extensively and I decided that both proposals would be accepted. It was essential for everyone to have access to electricity, a basic need in modern society. As it turned out later, the financial assessment of

---

*In the National sample survey (NSSO report of the 61st Round covering the period 2004–05, the share of households using electricity for lighting was 54.9 per cent. These surveys are held periodically to assess electricity usage.

the requirement of the programme was indeed highly understated by the Ministry of Power. But I let that go at that time. We today have an electrification of more than 85 per cent households. If we had delayed it then, maybe we would still have half the population living in darkness.

Institutional Reform

While these development initiatives were being taken, it was clear that institutional reforms were vital to ensuring effective delivery of services and reducing corruption. This area needed urgent attention. With the expansion of information technology (IT), it was clear that public services could be provided far more conveniently and efficiently through the use of the Internet. I was clear that if we could automate public services and remove the interface with a government official, corruption would be minimized. I decided to support efforts in this direction.

The CoS would meet regularly to discuss the progress achieved in twenty-seven sectors and services delivered at the district level, such as the issue of ration card and driving licence, copy of land records, registration of documents, the renewal or permission for construction of houses, and payment of fees. Intensive efforts were required by the states to adopt this mode of delivery of public services, especially since these were still the early days of e-governance. While some states had adopted it for a large number of public services, others were still only beginning to do so. In the meanwhile, the RTI Act had been adopted. This provided for all circulars issued by the government to be made available to the public, and all laws, rules, regulations and public documents be available in e-mode. This was applicable to all public offices and helped promote e-governance. However, even after more than a decade, there are many areas in various states where IT is still not being used for the delivery of public services.

One of the sectors that made good progress in providing services using IT was corporate governance. Since companies have to file a number of returns, the opening of a new business company would take months. This was gradually shifted to e-mode with the help of Tata Consultancy Services (TCS). It had great expertise in this area and a good track record. We began with an initial version of MCA-17, which later evolved to a very efficient model called MCA-21.

An area where we worked closely with various ministries was the issue of passports. The process was reviewed by a group under Vijay Sharma, additional secretary in the Cabinet secretariat (he later became the chief information commissioner, or CIC). A basic issue was clearance from the police, which took a lot of time and papers languished in its absence. I was of the view that a passport was every citizen's right and had nothing to do with good or bad police records. The IB and MHA found it difficult to accept such a radical shift. Finally, a process was initiated by the Ministry of External Affairs (MEA) to reduce problems due to delays in police clearances. This was the beginning of reforms in the issuing of passports. Since then, many changes have taken place, and most of the internal processes have been outsourced.

This was the time the World Bank took the initiative to rank countries on the ease of doing business. We realized that our systems needed major reforms. In the six key areas they were looking at—setting up a new company, closing a business, getting credit, getting an electricity connection, permissions for construction and implementation of a contract—there were too many steps involved and too much time taken for each step. Gradually, we have improved our systems by involving the states and trying to focus on each step. Some of these initiatives, taken by the NDA government, have enabled India to now feature in the top 100 countries in the ease of doing business.

Resolving Complex Issues

During my tenure, any issue that required coordination or assumption of leadership often called for my intervention. This included monitoring of prices, construction-work problems in the Commonwealth Games stadiums, the import and movement of wheat or pulses, keeping a close watch on issues such as the Baglihar Dam, which Pakistan threatened to stop construction on, resolving the Enron issue, which was plagued with international arbitration, and interacting with tough ministers on oil prices. The NAC, under Mrs Gandhi, was fairly active and would send various proposals to the government. Several of these were placed before the CoS for taking a view on.

In early 2005, an issue arose about the price of petroleum products. Sometime in early 2002, the oil pool mechanism had been dismantled and a market-based pricing system established. Under the old system, prices to producers of oil, such as the ONGC, were fixed administratively and a common fund of government-owned oil companies, such as the IOC, was established to keep prices of petrol and diesel at controlled rates. The oil companies were now free to fix the price of petroleum products, keeping the international market in mind. This was continued until about January–February 2004. Later, after the Lok Sabha elections, as the oil prices started rising, oil companies were forced to adjust the petrol and diesel prices to reflect the increased input costs. In oil refining, the major cost is of oil, and overall value addition is about 10 per cent. The year 2004 saw a continuous increase in international crude oil prices. Our refineries were importing more than 70 per cent of crude oil for making petrol and other oil products. The oil companies had no choice but to increase the price of diesel, etc. However, while the official decision was to give freedom to the oil companies to fix prices, the government informally advised them not to raise the prices further for petrol, diesel and liquefied petroleum gas (LPG), which were used by the common man. There were elections in some part or the other of the country all the time. An increase in the prices of these commodities was considered anti-people. But the oil companies had started incurring losses and were finding it increasingly difficult to make imports to meet domestic demand. The only way out was to increase the prices of petrol, diesel and LPG. Though the PM was in favour of this decision, all major constituents were against it. The issue was to be discussed in a meeting of ministers. The PM wanted me to explain the position to the railway minister.

When I met the minister, he was polite and there was no evidence of our earlier, rather sharp telephonic conversation on the question of the appointment of the railway-board member. I explained the international oil situation to him and said that if the selling prices of petrol and diesel in the domestic market were not increased, the oil companies would have no choice but to cut down on production. They did not have the resources to incur losses month after month. He observed that people would not like the increased prices of diesel in the rural areas during the elections, which were slated in Bihar a couple of months later. I pointed out that it was better to have the market fully supplied with diesel and petrol than low prices but huge shortages and black marketing. When the issue of petrol and diesel prices came up for discussion next time in the meeting of ministers, the railway minister did not oppose a proposal to increase the prices. When the PM remarked at this change in approach, he clarified that I had earlier fully explained to him the position and the available options.

But the nature of governance issues is not limited to complex internal problems. Several issues like Baglihar and Dabhol had international dimensions, and huge financial implications for us.

Baglihar

In 1960, India and Pakistan signed the Indus Waters Treaty on sharing the waters of the tributaries of the Indus river.* Under this treaty, the waters of the three western rivers, including the Chenab, were to be used exclusively by Pakistan and those of the three

---

*The Indus Waters Treaty was signed on 19 September 1960, with World Bank participation. Pandit Jawaharlal Nehru and Pakistani Field Marshal Ayub Khan were signatories for their respective countries. Article IX(2)(a) of the treaty mentions:
Article IX: Settlement of Differences and Disputes
(?) If the Commission does not reach an agreement on any of the questions mentioned in paragraph (1), then a difference will be deemed to have arisen, which shall be dealt with as follows:
(a) Any difference, which in the opinion of either Commissioner falls within the provision of Part 1 of Annexure F, shall at the request of either Commissioner be dealt with by a Neutral Expert in accordance with the provisions of Part 2 of Annexure F.

eastern rivers—the Sutlej, the Beas and the Ravi—were allocated to India. However, run-of-river projects were permitted, with limited pondage of water, with the help of a low-height dam for power generation. Both countries had appointed Indus Waters Treaty commissioners. Together they formed a permanent Indus Waters Commission, which was set up to ensure effective implementation of the treaty. The treaty provided a dispute-resolution mechanism.

The Baglihar Hydroelectric Power Project* was initially thought of by India in the early Nineties. After its sanction, work on the project started in 1999. The 900-megawatt (MW) project was aimed at power generation by building a run-of-river project on the Chenab. The project involved setting up three turbines for power generation in Phase I, and then again for a similar capacity in Phase II. In terms of the treaty, there were several limitations on project parameters.

While construction work on Phase I was on, talks with Pakistan continued in the annual round of their Indus Waters Commission. Pakistan felt that the project being built was in violation of the Treaty. The project was important for India, as it provided fuller utilization of the waters of the Chenab, and clean power in J&K, an acutely power-deficient state. Also, a lot of money had been spent on the project by the time Pakistani objections were fully considered, and India could not afford to let that investment go to waste. When no agreement was reached between the two commissioners, in January 2005 Pakistan invoked the provisions of the Treaty and approached the World Bank. Taking note of it, the World Bank appointed Raymond Lafitte, professor at the Swiss Federal Institute

---

*The broad facts of the project were obtained from various websites but primarily from South Asia Network on Dams, Rivers and People (SANDRP). Accessed 23 February 2018, http://www.sandrp.in/hydropower/Baglihar_Crucial_Facts_0207.pdf

of Technology of Lausanne (EPFL) as a neutral expert (NE).

Pakistan had several concerns about the project. It felt that the gates built in the dam for release of floodwater during rainy season were not at an appropriate height. Also, the gates provided near the bottom of the dam for flushing out silt were considered impermissible by it in terms of Treaty provisions, as these were below dead storage level (DSL), below which water could not go in terms of the treaty. Informally, Pakistan expressed the view that India could flood their downstream area by opening both types of gates. They considered it a serious security issue. They also felt that the dam was too high and that the large quantity of water stored in the dam was in violation of the Treaty, which had contemplated limited storage. There were some other issues too, related to the design of the dam.

India's main concern was that the project be financially viable on a long-term basis. It, therefore, had computed water storage and the consequent height of the dam to meet this parameter. It was particularly worried about the huge silt that accumulated in dams built in this region, as the mountain ranges were young. India's experience of the Salal dam was bad, as it got silted very early and had a sharply reduced power-generation capacity due to reduced water storage. India was therefore keen that the gates be built near the bottom of the dam to flush out silt during every rainy season. There were also issues related to the safety of the dam. During rainy season, there was heavy downpour and rivers overflowed. It was important to build an adequate number of gates at the proper height for the full discharge of floodwater. This would reduce pressure on the dam from floodwater and make it safe. India defended its design of the dam based on techno-economic requirements, which were permissible under the treaty.

The NE made extensive studies and presented his findings on the claims of the two countries on the design of the dam and its adherence to the provisions of the Indus Waters Treaty.* On the safety of the dam against floods, he broadly accepted the Indian claim that considering heavy rains in the region and past flood records of the river, the dam should have gates and spillways so that floodwater could be easily released and the safety of the dam assured. The NE argued that 89 per cent of more than 13,000 dams in the world that he had studied had a similar design. He also accepted India's concern about the need to protect the dam against accumulation of silt due to the fragile nature of the Himalayas. For this, he came out quite strongly in favour of the gates near the bottom of the dam for flushing out silt. This, he said, would ensure economical operation of the power plant and avoid damage to the turbines due to the passing of muddy water. He took note of the principle enunciated by the Chinese engineers: Store clear water and discharge muddy water. He rejected the Pakistani argument that lowering the water level below the DSL was a breach of the treaty, as, he argued, this was needed for the maintenance of the plant, which was permissible. The NE also broadly accepted the Indian contention on the amount of water to be stored in the dam. This was critical to power generation.

Broadly, while the approach of the Indian side was accepted, there were some marginal changes in the design. The NE changed

---

*The neutral expert report. Accessed 23 February 2018, http://siteresources. worldbank.org/SOUTHASIAEXT/Resources/223546-1171996340255/ BagliharSummary.pdf

the height of the outlet provided for outflow of water from the dam to the water channel for taking it to the turbines. While he brought it at the highest level as per the provisions of the Treaty, he also ensured that this did not result in damage to the turbines. Similarly, he partially conceded Pakistan's argument that the height of the freeboard (dam height above the pondage or the permitted level of full storage of water in the dam), which was 4.5 metres as per the design of the dam proposed by India, be reduced. Both these changes were not critical parameters for us.

The NE's determination and our successful argument before him had several positive features. We had taken the risk and gone ahead with the construction of the dam even as there were objections from Pakistan. The project got support from the NE determination, which paved the way for Phase II, leading to a 900-MW project. Our initial objective was thus effectively met.

Dabhol

The Dabhol power project*, which had been set up by Enron in the mid-'90s, had more than ₹10,000 crore of investment lying

---

*Details about the Dabhol power plant accessed from the following sources:
(i)https://www.power-technology.com/projects/dabhol-combined-cycle-power-plant-maharashtra-india/
(ii) 'Fact Sheet: Background on Enron's Dabhol Power Project', Minority Staff, Committee on Government Reform, US House of Representatives, 22 February 2002, accessed 25 March 2019
http://finance-mba.com/Dabhol_fact_sheet.pdf
(iii) Preeti Kundra, 'Notes: Looking Beyond the Dabhol Debacle: Examining Its Causes and Understanding Its Lessons', Vanderbilt Journal of Transnational Law, Vol. 41:907

idle for over five years. Also, India was getting involved in very costly international arbitration. This needed quick resolution. The project, however, had a murky history and was considered a monument of corruption. The awarding of the project to Enron was considered non-transparent and not done through competitive bidding. The cost of project per MW was much more than other projects. An Enron employee, Linda Powers, had testified before the US parliamentary committee that Enron had spent $20 million on 'educating Indians on how capitalist business should work'.* In the election campaign for the Maharashtra Assembly, which took place in early 1995, the opposition to the project, which was still only half built at that time, was very strong. Even the World Bank had been strongly opposed to it. In a letter in April 2003, sent by its India country director Heinz Vergin to the Government of India, it had refused to fund it on the grounds that the project was economically not viable, that it would produce too much power at too high a price for the state, that it was too large for base-load operations and that the power produced from LNG would cost much more than power from coal. Under the proposed deal, the plant would displace lower-cost power, raising power costs. The bank thought that it would place a heavy financial burden on the Maharashtra State Electricity Board (MSEB).

While I was looking for a resolution to the problem, I remembered my advice as joint secretary in the Ministry of Commerce to Sudhir Mulji, who was then chairman of the STC, about two decades back. Those days, the STC building was getting constructed

---

*'The Enron Affair—Shadowy Path to State Approval', *Financial Times*, 12 January 2002

right on Janpath in the heart of Delhi. Construction work on the building had stopped, as there had been a mishap and a part of the building under construction had fallen. There was a chorus for a vigilance inquiry. When Sudhir asked for my advice, I had mentioned to him that any delay in construction would escalate the cost of the building. If someone had indulged in corruption, they needed to be punished, but why stop the project? Sudhir needed to work on both these aspects independently—completion of the project and an inquiry to punish the guilty. He accepted my advice.

As I studied the Enron project further, I was clear that the best course of action was to make the investment work and settle outstanding arbitration and court cases. It gradually became clear that negotiation was the best option. The Dabhol Power Project was set up in Maharashtra to meet its energy needs. A delegation of the state government had gone to the US to invite investors and had had very fruitful discussions. In the summer of 1992, a team of the Enron Development Corporation (EDC) landed in India and followed up on its earlier discussions. This resulted in a Memorandum of Understanding (MoU) being signed between the MSEB, Enron and General Electric (GE) to set up a power plant. The overall capacity of the project was fixed at 2,015 MW. The company to be set up for establishing the plant and other facilities had 80 per cent share of Enron and 10 per cent each of the two US companies, GE and Bechtel Enterprises, Inc. While GE was to provide the machinery, Bechtel was to oversee the execution of the project. The plant was to run on LNG, which was to be imported. For this, a jetty, a breakwater to enable berthing of LNG tankers in all kinds of weather, and other infrastructure was to be set up. This was to be the first such plant in India.

After extensive negotiations, the parties agreed that of the power generated, 90 per cent was to be purchased by MSEB. The government of Maharashtra gave a state guarantee of payment of MSEB dues and the Government of India gave a counter guarantee up to $300 million for such payment. Of the total project cost of $2.8 billion, $1 billion was to be the equity shared by Enron, GE and Bechtel. The loans were gradually tied up with Overseas Private Investment Corporation (OPIC), US EXIM Bank, Bank of America, ANZ Grindlays Bank, ICICI and a number of other Indian and foreign banks.

While the project was still under implementation, it was decided that it would be done in two phases after a negotiated settlement with the new BJP-Shiv Sena government. The shareholding of Enron in the revised project was reduced by 30 per cent to be taken up by MSEB. Phase I of the 740-MW project was to run on naphtha (instead of LNG) to save on foreign exchange. Phase II, with 1,444 MW, was to run on LNG, as planned earlier. The total capacity was thus fixed at 2,184 MW. The first phase was completed in 1999.

It gradually became clear that the plant could not continue to run for long, as it was financially unsustainable for the MSEB and it could not afford to buy and pay such high costs for power. The MSEB initially did not make payments for the power purchased by it for the month of October. The following month, in view of its financial constraints, it decided to sell its stake in the Dabhol Power Company (DPC), reducing its shareholding to 15 per cent (from the 30 per cent offered to it). Considering that it was now becoming clear that a major policy shift was required, the Godbole Committee was formed to outline a possible direction for the project.

The committee reaffirmed that it was not possible for the MSEB to meet the payment obligations, as it involved taking on a very heavy financial burden. It suggested restructuring the project instead.

In view of pending payment defaults by the MSEB, the DPC now invoked the guarantee of the government of Maharashtra first and later of the Government of India. Meanwhile, the MSEB had given notice to the DPC, alleging violation of the terms of the power purchase agreement (PPA). While the government of Maharashtra advised against any such payment, the Government of India held that the 'conditions precedent' to the invoking of the guarantee had not been met. It rejected the claim of the DPC under its payment guarantee.

The DPC now moved for arbitration proceedings as provided in the PPA. The MSEB, however, cancelled the PPA and took several other steps to safeguard its interests. It petitioned the Maharashtra Electricity Regulatory Commission (MERC) to declare that it had cancelled the PPA validly. It also requested the commission to set the price for power. There was a special arrangement with Canara Bank for the payment of dues of the DPC. The MSEB requested that the DPC be barred from using it. The MSEB also decided not to purchase power from the DPC any further and informed them as such in May 2001. The MERC accepted the pleas of the MSEB and granted them relief. The DPC approached the Bombay High Court but got no favourable orders. Litigation in Indian courts was on in full swing at this juncture.

While the DPC did not have success in Indian courts, its promoters, Enron, GE and Bechtel, were trying other methods to realize the dues. The US administration considered this a symbol of India's foreign direct investment (FDI) regime and raised the issue several times. Once it was clear in early 2001 that the project could be cancelled, there were several meetings at the political level. Secretary of State Colin Powell raised the issue with our foreign minister. Subsequently, Vice President Dick Cheney spoke to Mrs Gandhi, who was then leader of the largest party in the Opposition. Later, in October 2001, senior US diplomat Alan Larson again raised the issue with our foreign minister and NSA. As part of its efforts, Kenneth Lay, CEO of Enron, sent a letter to the PM in September that year, offering to sell its stake for $2.3 billion, including $1.2 billion for its investment and $1.1 billion for the purchase of offshore lenders' debt. He maintained that his legal claim was much higher and was likely to be $4–5 billion. The issue was to be raised by President Bush in a meeting with PM Vajpayee, but Enron's debacle and financial mismanagement was announced a day before the scheduled talks.

After Enron's bankruptcy, the status of the DPC's ownership became unclear. The DPC was an unlimited liability company. Who would assume control and recover the monies due to various investors? In the meanwhile, in 2002 Indian banks approached the Bombay High Court to secure the assets created so far. Separately, OPIC, GE and Bechtel worked on an arrangement by which shares of Enron in the DPC were acquired by GE and Bechtel. This arrangement was approved by a New York bankruptcy court in 2004. Armed with this, GE and Bechtel filed arbitration proceedings under the India-Mauritius Bilateral Investment Treaty provisions. Other foreign banks also moved towards arbitral proceedings. A claim of $6 billion was filed before the arbitration court in London. While the project languished, litigation was on in full flow.

When the issue reached me, we had two challenges—how to

settle the litigation and how to utilize the assets for generating power at affordable prices. The PM had set up an empowered group of ministers (EGoM) to oversee the decisions to be taken for the project. Primarily, however, I had to work out a strategy to resolve the two issues. Clearly, the loans had to be restructured. Also, the control of the plant had to come to us. It was decided to set up a company, Ratnagiri Gas and Power Private Limited (RGPPL), in the name of the district where the plant was located. By now, an Indian company had set up an LNG terminal, and GAIL had acquired good expertise in the area. National Thermal Power Corporation Limited, or NTPC Limited, had a large number of thermal power plants and had experience running them. GAIL and NTPC were the natural choice for undertaking the revival. Both of them put in matching equity while setting up the new company. As we started work on financial restructuring, we kept a major objective in mind—that the settlement had to result in power costs that were saleable. Without this, the exercise would have little value.

But before the new company could take over the facilities, there had to be a one-time settlement of all the outstanding claims of a large number of stakeholders. M. Damodaran was heading the Industrial Development Bank of India (IDBI) and initiated the process. In view of past problems, India was not being taken seriously those days. He persevered and achieved the first breakthrough in January 2005. Later, when different banks fell in line, ANZ Grindlays gave it a tough time. In fact, Damodaran once jocularly remarked that while the negotiations were difficult, drinking one cup of coffee after another as discussions went on over prolonged periods was even more painful.

Kalpana J. Morparia, who was the joint managing director

of ICICI, led the discussions later with other institutions. As negotiations proceeded, it was clear that OPIC, GE and Bechtel had a very close-knit bond and were giving the negotiators a tough time. GE and Bechtel had their own shares, as well as those acquired from Enron. A settlement with them was required to get the Dabhol assets transferred to the new company. There were claims against the DPC for work done by contractors which had to be settled. Once the lenders were agreed the assets could be transferred by orders of the Debts Recovery Tribunal in India, OPIC and US EXIM bank support was needed to swing the deal. Gradually, the Indian team was able to separate OPIC's interest and bring it to settle its claims. This was a major breakthrough. The team next worked on GE. They had large interests in India as the power equipment manufacturer. They had shown keen interest in several power plants that the NTPC was planning to build. The negotiating team informally sent word that unless they were more forthcoming, it would be difficult to look at their offer with positive interest in other areas. GE finally realized the futility of non-cooperation. It took about three months to convince them. Bechtel was the most difficult party. It took its own time, and some backchannel efforts were needed to finally bring them around.

The team worked on several other claims too. Dabhol had signed a sale and purchase agreement for LNG with two companies in Oman and Abu Dhabi for the supply of 2.1 million tonnes of LNG annually for a period of twenty years. The MSEB was a signatory of this. An agreement for chartering an LNG tanker, Laxmi, had also been signed by the DPC with Greenfield Shipping Company Limited for transporting the LNG fuel from these two countries. There were financial obligations under it too. Since neither had the LNG been lifted nor the transport tanker used, there were claims against the DPC and the MSEB. These claims had to be extinguished before the new company could start functioning.

While financial restructuring was being looked at, the operation of the plant had to be ensured. It was closed for about four years, though some maintenance was being done. We soon realized that while all the plant designs were with us, a key was required to make it work. We did not have that key. Hence, even after the financial settlement with GE and Bechtel, we required their continued support to run the plant. Also, the LNG terminal had to be made operational. A decision was also required for the breakwater. It had not been built so far. Without it, the worry was that we could lose nearly six months for imports of LNG, as the sea in that period would be too rough to permit the docking of the LNG tankers.

To make the power produced saleable, we had to work on a strategy. The cost of LNG in the international market was very high, so we had to get some source. LNG being imported by Petronet from Qatar was cheap but was already tied up. The Reliance gas fields in the Krishna-Godavari basin were low-cost but pipeline infrastructure for getting it was required to be put in place. The gas pipeline to connect Dahej with Mumbai and down to Ratnagiri and onwards to Karnataka and Kerala was needed anyway. GAIL was to lay down the pipeline as part of its plan to develop a national grid. As GAIL started work on laying pipelines, it encountered difficulties. The pipeline was to pass through two states—Gujarat and Maharashtra. In Gujarat, it was slated to pass through the farm of a former Union minister. He was unrelenting and opposed to it. Work stopped at the site.

Finally, I recall contacting Narendra Modi, then chief minister of the state, to settle the issue. He was extremely helpful.

We worked through many of these issues as I met the stakeholders from the Indian side and monitored progress of the work. We had the strong support of the government of Maharasthra in resolving the issue. Our negotiations of restructuring continued for nearly six months. Finally, in October 2005, we had it in place—a solution that led to the closure of about a dozen court cases and a financial settlement on which nearly a dozen and a half bankers and other financial institutions agreed. Everyone made concessions to arrive at this solution. While not much was known about it in the press, Sucheta Dalal, a leading commentator on financial matters, wrote:

> However, in a move that redeems past mischief, the Government of India needs to be complimented for a hard negotiation that stitched together a viable deal to revive the massive 2,150 MW combined cycle power plant and 5 MTPA LNG facility. The process of reviving Dabhol was considered so impossibly expensive and un-negotiable that some NGOs had even suggested that it should be converted into a monument to political corruption.*

As the final settlement was placed before the Union Cabinet, I explained the details as per normal Cabinet practice. Pranab

---

*Sucheta Dalal, 'How the Dabhol deal was swung by the govt', Suchetadalal.com, 10 October 2005, accessed 17 March 2019
http://www.suchetadalal.com/?id=86289acd-0b92-ece8-492e83f4abb4&base=sub_sections_content&f&t=How+the+Dabhol+deal+was+swung+by+the+govt

Mukherjee, who had chaired the EGoM, made a few comments, and then, turning to the PM, paid handsome compliments to my leadership during the entire process. Foreign Minister Natwar Singh remarked that while the Cabinet could take note of it, 'we should also pass a resolution complimenting the Cabinet secretary'. This suggestion was approved.

Commenting on the process, Sucheta Dalal in her article observed:

> The key player in the Dabhol negotiations turned out to be Cabinet Secretary B.K. Chaturvedi. An important negotiating team member recalls, 'The Cabinet Secretary's leadership was outstanding—great conceptual clarity, attention to detail and persuasive ability. He shot down bureaucratic objections and saw the point about finding a solution soon.*

At another point she wrote:

> Chaturvedi never directly invoked the might of government, but knew exactly which buttons to push in order to get results. Power Secretary R.V. Shahi, who knows the inner working and financing of power projects, played a crucial role and the Defence Minister and the Law Minister also chipped in with important suggestions.**

This was the first phase of Dabhol's reinventing itself. While we had done away with the $6-billion arbitration and others cooking in the pipeline, the problem of the impact of increasing LNG prices

---

*Ibid
**Ibid

in the international market and difficulties that could arise during the course of the actual operation of the power plant had to be addressed in the next several years. During the next few years, the new company looked at these issues. Things gradually fell in place, especially when gas was allotted to it from the Reliance gas fields of the Krishna-Godavari basin. During 2007–09, the company finally achieved the commercial working of plants for nearly 2,000 MW. It earned profits for three years. But since then, it has not been able to get the gas. Due to high prices of LNG, this power is not acceptable to state electricity boards (SEBs). Like a large number of other gas-based power plants, RGPPL is suffering. It is waiting for a new policy intervention that will revive LNG-based power plants. Meanwhile, it is supplying power to the railways. But it has a lot of spare capacity. I understand it is working on the separation of the LNG terminal and restructuring of the power plant. But unless problems of gas-based power plants in the country gets resolved—most of them are either closed or running at very low capacity, leading to losses—RGPPL will continue to suffer.

Chapter 5

HANDLING EMERGENCIES

D isasters of different natures have traditionally been dealt with in our country by the state governments, and their efforts to provide relief and rehabilitation have been supported by the MHA. In the past two decades, the nature of such response and preparedness has undergone a change. The nature of problems is no more traditional. To floods, droughts and cyclones have been added chemical weapons, nuclear weapons, terrorism and tsunamis. In all national emergencies, the National Crisis Management Committee (NCMC) is called into operation immediately. This is presided over by the Cabinet secretary and includes the secretaries of the ministries of home affairs and defence, apart from others. Secretary RAW, director IB, the three service chiefs and secretaries of other departments are invited, depending upon the nature of the emergency.

This institutional arrangement was very much in place on that fateful day of 26 December 2004, when the Indian Ocean tsunami struck. In all disasters, the first responder is the state government and the district administration. In these days of fast communication, as information reaches the Central government, it gets in touch with states and coordinates relief operations. The events related to the tsunami disaster provide an excellent example of the seamless fashion in which India handles disasters.

When Tsunami Strikes

It was a wintry Sunday morning of the day after Christmas in 2004. Though my job required me to work round the clock, I felt a little relaxed on that day. There was no crisis looming on the horizon. I decided to spend some time on the golf course early in the morning. Before I could move to the third hole, I got a call on my mobile phone. The shipping minister was on the line from Chennai. He mentioned a serious problem at the port and that the water level in the sea was rising rapidly with massive waves. He called it a 'tsunami'*.

I apologized to my partner on the course and promptly left for home. In between, I got more facts and called up my staff officer to fix an emergency meeting of the Crisis Management Group (CMG). The first task was to make an assessment of the situation.

---

*Tsunami was not a word in our lexicon. It had its origins in Japan and was then adopted by the world. It was formed from two Japanese characters indicating 'harbour' and 'waves', and was commemorated in the nineteenth century woodblock print by Hokusai. In literal translation, it meant harbour wave with two kanji characters: 'tsu' meaning 'harbour' and 'nami' meaning 'wave'. The word dates back more than 1,000 years, as most tsunamis occurred in only that country. These massive waves had occurred mostly in the Pacific Ocean as it is ringed by so many volcanoes and craters. This fencing by earthquake zones under the sea bed had produced many tsunamis over the decades.

The PM had to be urgently briefed.

As the CMG sat down to discuss the issue, the air chief was very worried. They had an air base at Andaman and Nicobar Islands. It seemed that the massive sea waves had overrun half the base right in front of the officers. Many air force personnel had died. The full extent of the damage was yet to be assessed. A Dornier aircraft had already taken off from the air base in Orissa (now Odisha) to get more facts. Two An-32 aircraft had left the air base in Tamil Nadu for a similar recce.

Gradually, as discussion proceeded, the unprecedented scale of the tragedy became evident. The task was clearly to first reach those marooned and give them food, water and shelter. In the Andaman and Nicobar archipelago, there were a number of islands which, according to the first information reaching us, had been completely cut off. An immediate task was to provide transport and communication network to enable full-scale relief operations there. We set up a small group to act as a focal point for meeting these basic requirements. It acted as a core group for the next three months, had operating-level officers and was supported by naval ships, Coast Guard boats, Indian Airlines aircraft and air force transport aircraft. Supported by this group, we could organize the movement of paramilitary and army units to the islands and affected areas in the states of Tamil Nadu, Kerala, Andhra Pradesh and Pondicherry (now Puducherry), and provide immediate relief in coordination with the MHA. Simultaneously, we asked the MHA to be in touch with all affected state governments, to support and organize full-scale relief operations.

The Cabinet met the next day and a Cabinet committee under the PM was formed to oversee all relief efforts. It met regularly for several months and discussed efforts being made for relief, areas that needed special attention, and policy and financial aid required by the states.

Since it was holiday season, there was a huge influx of tourists. A large number of tourists were left stranded, as there was heavy damage to the runway at Port Blair, the capital of the Andaman and Nicobar Islands. Only about 5,000 feet of it was usable. This, however, enabled smaller-sized aircraft to land and take off. We mounted an elaborate evacuation operation. Over the next five days, we evacuated more than 6,300 persons by air back to the mainland. Indian Airlines, which was tasked with this responsibility, sent regular flights to the affected areas. During this period, the airlines mounted more than sixty flights—almost eight to ten flights every day. It was heart-warming, even in this season of tragedy, to see the successful completion of these operations in less than a week.

Scale of the Tragedy

The loss of human lives on the Andaman and Nicobar Islands was initially estimated to be 2,000. There was, however, a long list of missing persons. Of the 5,000–6,000 individuals reported missing from all over the country, most were from these islands. The loss was particularly severe in the Nicobar group of islands, including among tribes such as the Onge, the Jarawa, the Shompen and the Sentinelese. When the disaster struck, many of them moved to higher lands. The lighthouse on the Great Nicobar Island had several people trapped in it as the tsunami waves engulfed it.

There was massive damage to infrastructure. The telecommunication and power lines were damaged, leading to a severe disruption in power supply and mobile connectivity. Lighthouses, roads, culverts, jetties and fishing boats were either washed away or damaged and non-functional. The ingress of sea water on the islands had affected freshwater sources. Dead bodies were strewn on many islands. There was need for strong medical relief. On mainland India, Tamil Nadu and Kerala were the worst affected, apart from Pondicherry. Andhra Pradesh had comparatively less damage. More than 8,000 people were dead, about 300 people had gone missing and nearly 500 children had become orphans. Rescue, shelter, food, livelihood, restoration of infrastructure and medical rehabilitation of orphaned children were some of the challenges met by the state government with Central-government support.

The unprecedented disaster required a quick briefing of all political parties. They had to be sensitized to the efforts being made by the government and the extent of the tragedy, particularly since 'tsunami' was not a word known to many. The home secretary was tasked with this responsibility. It was decided to bring in sharp focus the extent of the tragedy, the scale of efforts required and the action which was under way to bring relief to the affected areas. The parties responded positively to the approach of the Central government in handling the issue.

Massive Rescue and Relief Operations

Relief operations included locating living persons and providing them shelter immediately. In a number of islands, the population was small and providing relief was a problem. They were sent by boat or air to relief camps in the Andaman islands, which had lesser damage and were easily approachable. Approaching the tribes was a difficult task. They had moved to higher land and were not inclined to accepting support. In mainland Tamil Nadu and Kerala, the relief camps were located in school buildings; temporary shelters were also made. In these camps there was provision for food and medicines.

The relief operations in the Andaman and Nicobar Islands required extensive support from naval ships, boats, helicopters and medical supply. Power lines had to be restored quickly and generation started. This required a continuous supply of diesel. Water resources had to be located in several areas where these had been damaged. Until then, supply of fresh water had to be arranged. Telecommunications had been damaged badly, and in each of the islands we put in extra equipment so that communication was up and functioning. A major issue was disposing of dead bodies, which were strewn all over the smaller islands in the Nicobar group. The problem was particularly acute in Tamil Nadu. We made special efforts and sent a group from Mumbai to assist the efforts of the Tamil Nadu government.

Relief efforts were launched on a massive scale. More than 2,100 personnel from the Border Security Force (BSF), Indo Tibetan Border Police (ITBP), Rapid Action Force (RAF), Central Reserve Police Force (CRPF) and Central Industrial Security Force (CISF), and about 20,000 Army, Navy, Air Force and Coast Guard officials were involved in this huge operation. The armed forces deployed forty ships, forty-two helicopters and thirty-four fixed-wing aircraft. Defence forces evacuated civilians from Sri Lanka and the Maldives too, apart from nearly 6 lakh persons rescued in mainland India and the Andaman and Nicobar Islands. About 400 relief camps were set up where affected persons were brought in for relief. The relief efforts were supported by a number of NGOs. Satellite telephones, the Army and the police communication network and equipment installed for restoring communication by Bharat Sanchar Nigam Limited (BSNL) were all used to maintain uninterrupted network. Several points were identified for the lifting of food, water, medicines, tents, torches, diesel generator (DG) sets and other relief material. As a policy, it was not considered necessary to ask any international agency for aid. On the contrary, we even provided support to Sri Lanka and the Maldives, which had been badly hit by the tsunami.

All the affected states required doctors urgently. The need was particularly acute in the Andaman and Nicobar Islands. There were very few doctors available locally who could be sent to the islands. It was gradually met by roping in doctors from the mainland. The supply of medicines and other equipment, too, was quickly supplemented. Many of the doctors were required at relief camps, but a number of them were also needed to look after the children and the women in other areas.

Tsunami Management Response

The massive relief and mitigation efforts required in the aftermath of the tsunami made us realize the need for a more dedicated organization that could be committed to working for mitigation, prevention and rescue and relief operations. It was also considered necessary to have the structure right up to the district level. We enacted a law called the Disaster Management Act, 2005, to provide for the setting up of a National Disaster Management Authority (NDMA), presided over by the PM with a number of members, including a vice chairman.

The authority was tasked with the responsibility of preparing plans for handling different aspects of disasters, including prevention, mitigation, rescue, relief, planning, capacity-building and the setting up of a National Disaster Response Force (NDRF) trained for handling disaster management. The Act also provided for the setting up of disaster-management committees at the state and district level. A national disaster-management fund was also set up. Simultaneously, a National Disaster Management Authority was established, with the PM as its chairman. Its first vice chairman was the former Chief of the Army Staff General N.C. Vij. He put the authority on a strong footing and organized the structure and details well. NDMA has now become an effective responder in many disasters. However, the same cannot be said for the state-level authorities. There is a need to prepare plans for meeting and mitigating disasters. A few years back, courts had to remind the states of their lack of preparedness in this regard. While relief-and-rescue was the first response during tsunami management, the second phase was providing infrastructure for the population that had lost its fishing boats, nets and other equipment, providing homes to hundreds of children who had become orphans, especially in Tamil Nadu, where the damage was huge, undertaking treatment of lands ravaged by sea water to ensure cultivation and livelihood, providing permanent housing for many who had become homeless, and putting the transport and communication infrastructure back in shape. It was an opportunity to develop preventive measures against future natural disasters and putting in place a tsunami warning system for states in the Indian Ocean, quite like the one existing for states in the Pacific Ocean, including Japan and the US.

Permanent and long-term rehabilitation required financial resources. This was beyond the financial capacity of the states. The Central government provided the initial funds for this and, later, after a fuller evaluation of the needs of each state, funds from the World Bank, the ADB and the Centre's own resources were pooled in to meet the needs of the states. The total resources tied up for this support were about ₹10,000 crore. For the Andaman and Nicobar Islands, which were a direct responsibility of the Central government, we put up a special package for immediate relief. This covered assistance for both temporary and permanent shelters, support to fishermen who had been the hardest hit in terms of employment and loss of shelter, setting infrastructure back up, and agriculture and relief operations.

When disaster struck, questions were raised about the lack of any warning of the impending disaster. No initiatives had been taken earlier to have a collaboration among the countries along the Indian Ocean to develop a tsunami warning system, as against the twenty-six countries in the Pacific Ocean rim. One of the reasons for the absence of a tsunami warning system among the countries along the Indian Ocean was that the region did not have a history of such massive earthquakes under the sea that could cause tsunamis.

Nevertheless, this triggered an initiative which resulted in the development of a tsunami warning system over the next five years in this region too. As a policy, it was decided that this would not be part of any particular system of any state in the Indian Ocean, but an independent system developed by India with the cooperation of other countries and UN agencies. The Indian Tsunami Early Warning System consists of seismic stations, tsunami buoys and tide gauges. Seven tsunami buoys are placed strategically in the

Indian Ocean at the Andaman-Sumatra-Makran zone, a place where the tectonic plates of the Earth's crust meet. This zone is highly susceptible to earthquakes. These buoys are equipped with bottom pressure recorders that transmit data on a real-time basis to the centre at Hyderabad. With this, the centre issues advisories to the MHA, the NDMA and state- and district-level management centres for follow-up action. With the establishment of this mechanism, we can get warnings of any incoming tsunami fifteen minutes to two hours earlier on the eastern coast of the country and about four hours earlier on the western coast.

Tremors in J&K

Memories of the devastating tsunami were still fresh when another disaster struck in J&K in early October next year. It was an earthquake of the intensity of 7.6 on the Richter scale, one of the biggest to have hit the region. The epicentre was about 19 km north-east of Muzaffarabad, the capital of PoK. The major areas affected were the three border districts of Poonch, Kupwara and Baramulla. Uri and Tangdhar, which were close to the centre of the earthquake, suffered severe damage. More than 1,000 people died and there was massive loss of infrastructure in the form of houses, power lines, roads and telecommunication. To make things worse, this happened close to the winter months, which, in these parts, are severe, with temperatures dipping below freezing point. While permanent housing would take some time to set up, it was necessary to provide temporary relief to protect the people from severe cold. The human aspect of the tragedy was hard to ignore. Many families in PoK had their relations in J&K and had to meet each other quickly to assess how much of the family was intact. The two governments realized this and mutually agreed to open five points on the Line of Control (LoC) in J&K where people could cross over from both sides to meet. Terrorist organizations in Pakistan saw this as an opportunity to befriend people of the region and strengthen their terrorist base. We started getting reports that terrorist organizations such as the JeM and the LeT had started some relief work for the people in PoK to further strengthen their base. It was reported that the Taliban had suspended their terror operations temporarily.

Immediately after the disaster struck, the NCMC met to take stock of the situation and work out a relief and rehabilitation support strategy in the region. The first responder in all disasters is the state government. Here, too, it started relief operations in J&K. The national crisis-management group under me would meet regularly to review the relief operations, and the financial and physical resources needed. The resident commissioner of J&K was a special invitee so we could gauge the state government's requirements quickly and see how the aid was reaching it. The Army, the Air Force and the paramilitary forces were asked to undertake massive relief operations using their physical presence in the region. The transportation of goods, food and relief material was undertaken on a war footing. In the border villages, army units decided to adopt selected areas for the development of schools and roads. We had regular interaction with the state officials and provided all the support we could. This region of the J&K-Afghanistan axis is highly prone to earthquakes. The PM knew this well. While he was on a visit to Malaysia in the second week of December that year to address a conference of the nations of the region, he saw a TV news ticker which mentioned another earthquake in the region. I received a call from the PM at 3.30 in the morning. Generally, it would be me who would call up the PM on his foreign visits to apprise him of developments in the country and brief him on issues so he could be in touch with events at home. Subbu said that the PM wanted to talk to me. 'Chaturvediji, there has been another earthquake in the Kashmir region, according to television news here. What are the details?' Dr Singh enquired.

I was a bit foxed. There were no reports with me of any such disaster. The previous evening there had been reports of some earthquake activity in Assam of the intensity of about 4 or 5 on the Richter scale. These tremors had caused no loss. I informed him about it but promised to get back to him after rechecking if there indeed had been any earthquake in the Kashmir region. I rang up the home secretary and asked him whether he knew of any such earthquake. The US Geological Service had reported this.

After some time, the home secretary came back with full facts, having spoken to the chief secretary of J&K. There had been seismic activity deep inside the Hindukush mountains. This had caused some damage in Afghanistan and some parts of Pakistan. It had had no impact on Indian areas. In the meanwhile, I had spoken to the joint secretary in the Cabinet secretariat and asked him to ascertain the facts as well. He had checked the position with the district commissioner of the state's border districts to assess the damage, if any, on the ground. The response of the field authority was interesting. 'No sir, there is no loss here. In any case, after the October earthquake, there is nothing left to destroy,' he had said.

The Day Mumbai Was Submerged

Mumbai gets a lot of rains in July and August. The Brihanmumbai Municipal Corporation (BMC) is usually prepared for it. But 2005 was different—26 July was a watershed in the history of the city. It received 39 inches of rain in a twenty-four-hour period. In view of the torrential rains in such a short time and the drains being unable to discharge water due to high tide in the sea, the water level rose on the streets and the suburban rails, disrupting transport services. Mumbai is heavily dependent on the suburban rail system and people walked for hours to get home. The city's transport system had broken down completely. Because of water on the railway lines, the operations of the western and central railways had to be shut down. The communication system, too, broke down, and mobile phones stopped functioning. The complete breakdown of mobile services and the non-availability of power to keep the mobile towers operational emphasized the need for renewable energy, and not diesel generator sets, as a resource in the city. The state government and civic agencies were not ready to meet this challenge, and the floods had a death toll of about 5,000.

Late in the evening, I got a call from the PM. He sounded very upset. Disturbing reports from Mumbai were constantly reaching him. I promised to speak to the then CM of Maharashtra, Vilasrao Deshmukh, to see what the specific needs of the city were and ensure effective support of all Central agencies to the state government. That day coincided with the farewell function of a former defence secretary. When I asked for an urgent meeting of the NCMC, I specifically mentioned that the naval chief should attend it. When we met around 10 p.m., all the service chiefs had joined the discussion, along with the home secretary and a number of other secretaries. I then rang up the CM and informed him of the PM's concern and his direction to go all out to support relief efforts in the state. I specifically mentioned naval infrastructure support. The next three days were bad for Mumbai. Rail operations and communications improved gradually, but it took some time to get back to normalcy.

Evacuation across Borders

While the 2004 tsunami, and the J&K earthquake and the massive Mumbai rains of 2005 posed challenges caused by natural disasters, the evacuation challenge in 2006 had a different dimension. It was a rescue operation designed to provide support to those persons, mostly Indian citizens, who were caught in the war-like zone of Lebanon-Israel.

Tension in West Asia between Israel and its neighbours has been a constant feature of the geopolitics of the region. But tensions escalated after the formation of Hezbollah, a militant group and political party in Lebanon. Sometime in early 2006, Hezbollah abducted two Israeli soldiers. This led to serious tension in the area. The Israelis started bombarding Lebanese positions, and there was a naval blockade of the Lebanese coast. With escalating tensions, the Indian embassy in Lebanon evacuated families of its staffers, as it was becoming a dangerous conflict zone and lives were in danger. This evacuation was done via neighbouring Syria. The families travelled by road to Syria and then from its capital, Damascus, undertook an onward journey to India. But this was worrisome, for there were about 12,000 Indians living in Lebanon then, and many were scared for their lives. There were also a large number of residents from other South Asian countries, the US and Europe who wanted to be evacuated.

The foreign secretary and the chief of naval staff (CNS) discussed the situation with me on 18 July. It was clear that the conflict was escalating and that we had to save the lives of all those Indian families who felt unsafe. Time was of the essence, as travel by road was getting increasingly dangerous. We decided to use the naval route. The CNS informed us that several of his ships were in the Mediterranean Sea region for naval exercises, and that they were returning and could be used for the Lebanon evacuation. There were, however, several risks, for which we had to be adequately prepared. The decision had to be taken immediately, as our ships would be entering the Suez Canal any time, and once they did, their return would be time-consuming. Traffic was only one-way and the movement was strictly controlled by Egyptian port authorities. The width of the canal was small and did not permit any U-turns. Any delay in decision-making would, therefore, render the evacuation plan unworkable as the increased strife in the area would make it risky. Our ships were going to be involved in a humanitarian exercise and we were worried they might get caught in the crossfire between Israel and Lebanon.

Meanwhile, our ships had heard a lot of messages and communication chatter. There were clear indications that Israel was going to put a blockade on the Lebanese port. The ships had started returning to avoid getting caught in the conflict. It was only on the morning of 17 July—when the task force, or our group of naval ships, was just short of the Great Bitter Lake in the Suez Canal, where the southbound convoys anchored to permit passage to the northbound convoys—that they got the message to return and help the evacuation process.

The naval ships were conscious of the field position. We had to bring all Indian families leaving Lebanon by bus to Beirut port to board the naval ships. This journey by road was risky—any of the buses carrying the returning Indians could be attacked. Also, in such disturbed conditions, many of them had lost their papers and had to be given temporary documents. Coordination was required with Cyprus authorities. Our High Commissioner in Cyprus and ambassador for Lebanon needed to be in close touch with the local authorities and the government of Israel. We needed an understanding so that the exchange of fire between Hezbollah and Israel could be temporarily stopped when the evacuation process was going on. We worked out a plan so that those wishing to be evacuated could be helped by the Indian embassy and moved to Beirut. Ships of the Indian Navy were then to be used to evacuate them to Larnaca, the neighbouring port of Cyprus. Air India was then expected to bring them back to Delhi. We discussed all aspects of the evacuation and decided to go ahead with it. We could not afford to wait. I briefed the PM on it.

Even after formal communication, there were several issues that needed to be sorted out to make the operation go smoothly. The Israeli naval blockade commanders had to be contacted to get entry to the area and reach Beirut port. As our ships would enter the blockade zone, the fleet of buses carrying those who needed to be evacuated would also simultaneously have to reach Beirut port to make the operation seamless. This required constant liaison with the local authorities. This was important, as many of the people being evacuated from Lebanon did not have complete travel documents. Immigration and security issues had to be sorted out. The problem was compounded as coordination with the Lebanese port authority was required and getting to them was a problem. Considering that more than 2,000 people were coming to board the ships, extensive arrangements were required for the journey.

Even as the ships entered the blockade area, a number of preparatory activities took place. Air India was contacted and asked to provide an adequate number of flights to Cyprus. Our High Commissioner there was in touch with the authorities to enable a quick issue of visas to the Air India crew. Since Air India did not operate from that airport, bays were allotted to them for parking and operations, with quick intervention from the embassy. Also, since getting visas for so many people travelling via Cyprus was not acceptable to their government under the European Union (EU) system, a novel system of transit slips was evolved. This would enable a transfer of passengers straight from the naval ships to the Air India aircraft.

Our preparations paid off and the evacuation process went smoothly, and was well appreciated by both the NRIs and neighbouring Sri Lanka and Nepal, whose citizens were also brought home by the Air India flights. Nearly 2,300 individuals were evacuated. It indicated the effectiveness of our system in emergencies. Neelam Sabharwal, who was then High Commissioner of India to Cyprus, later recalled to me, 'India's evacuation operation via Cyprus was considered as best coordinated and most efficient by the government of Cyprus, foreign correspondents, diplomats and international organizations. In fact, it was described a role model for the EU and other nations to emulate.'

The Navy saw this as a massive operation and summed it up as follows:

The Beirut sealift by the Western Fleet Ships thus brought home 2,280 people to safety, including 1,764 Indian nationals, besides nationals from Nepal, Sri Lanka, Lebanon and two Indian-origin citizens of the United States... Evacuation of so many people through ships designed for war required creation of huge amount of space for the passengers within the ships and dislocation of the existing officers and sailors on board to most inhospitable places in the ships. The dinner service for so many people on board warship was a sight to see. People were eating and sleeping in helicopter hangars and decks. Ladies and children were accommodated in sleeping cabins of sailors.*

---

*'Indian Navy: Like A Bridge on Troubled Waters... Op Sukoon', *Sainik Samachar*, accessed 22 February 2019
http://www.sainiksamachar.nic.in/englisharchives/2006/sep16-06/h5.htm

Chapter 6

REFLECTIONS ON THE PLANNING ERA

M y time as Cabinet secretary was going to end in mid-June 2007. The appointment of K.M. Chandrasekhar as my successor had already been approved. This time there was no glitch. I called on the PM sometime in early June. During my meeting, he enquired about my plans after superannuation. I told him frankly that I had no specific assignment in mind and was looking forward to some rest after more than four decades of continuous work. I also mentioned to him that my daughter and granddaughter had moved to India from the US and were staying with me. I was in no position to move out of Delhi. He did not comment. A day before my superannuation, he called me and enquired whether I would like to work as a member of the Planning Commission. The assignment involved reading, writing and policymaking. I liked all three. It traditionally had the rank of a minister of state. I thanked him and gave my consent.

Immediately after finishing my term as Cabinet secretary, I joined the Planning Commission. The PM was the chairman of the commission. It had eight full-time members, including Deputy Chairman Montek Singh Ahluwalia. The then secretary to the commission was of the rank of a member too. I joined as the ninth member. The commission in the initial years of planning had four to six full-time members. Later this increased to about seven or eight. I felt it was a bit crowded. Every member had a few states and a sector allotted to him. I was given all the eight states of the Northeast, UP and Chhattisgarh. I was also in charge of power as the sectoral allocation area. The work was not as cut out as in my earlier job. It took me some time to adjust.

The discussions in the Planning Commission were initially a bit of a cultural shock. During my discussions in the Cabinet secretariat, every participant would express their views. I would listen to them and then take a final decision. There were no further arguments. In the commission, however, members would express their views and, after the deputy chairman took a final view, the issue would start getting debated again. Often I got the feeling that I had become part of a debating society. Montek believed in freedom of discussion, but I felt this freedom was being taken to ridiculous lengths. Invariably, the final decision would take quite some time, as the members continued to put forward their views.

The Initial Years

The period that I joined coincided with the start of the Eleventh Five-Year Plan. The draft of the plan document had almost become final. There was very little scope for tinkering with it. The document was to be placed before the full Planning Commission for approval, and thereafter, the National Development Council (NDC) was to give its final seal of approval. I left the draft of the power sector almost intact, with just a few minor changes. The document had a rather ambitious target for setting up new power-generation capacities. But because of the huge demand gap and large unfulfilled needs for electricity, especially in rural areas, I supported the plan.

A few months after I joined, there was a meeting of the full Planning Commission. This was presided over by the PM and included, among others, Montek, all the full-time members, (including me), a number of Cabinet ministers who had been nominated by the PM as part-time members, and a few officials. The principal secretary to the PM was a special invitee. This was an occasion to present in brief the Eleventh Plan document and seek approval from the Planning Commission. While there were comments from members, especially Dr C. Rangarajan, who was chairman of the PM's Economic Advisory Council, there was a broad level of support for the plan. There was, however, a worry whether there would be enough financial resources in the coming years to fund all the schemes which were part of the plan. The Planning Commission invariably had a resource problem. The size of the plan based on the state's needs and the Central ministries' schemes was large. There were ambitious interventions such as MGNREGA, the Pradhan Mantri Gram Sadak Yojana (or the Prime Minister's Rural Roads Scheme), the universalizing of education, the NRHM, and infrastructure development in power, railways, shipping and airports. Additional resources were always required for the states of the Northeast and J&K. I thought it a bit strange that while the Eleventh Plan had already commenced from April that year, the full Planning Commission and the NDC—a body presided over by the PM and including Central Cabinet ministers, CMs, administrators of Union territories and all the ministries of the Government of India, apart from a host of other invitees—had still not approved it.

The meeting of the NDC took place later in 2007, in the third week of December, to approve the plan. Considering that the body was so large, the approach after the opening observations by the PM and the deputy chairman was for the CMs to speak, who invariably read their written speeches. The interventions from the Central ministers were brief and more pointed. States generally used the occasion to mention how well they were doing in various developmental areas and raised issues related to support required from the Centre to move forward. A constant refrain from many CMs present was that Centrally sponsored schemes be abolished and the money transferred to their budget for use as the state may decide. The Northeastern states were opposed to this, as they got a lot of support from these schemes and substantial extra resources from the Planning Commission's special window. The problem was that health and education indicators were poor in many states across the country. There continued to be widespread unemployment and underemployment in rural areas. Agriculture research and extension needed strong support. There were a number of states that had a poor resource base and could not provide enough money on infrastructural projects such as rural housing and roads. So while a number of schemes at that time needed to be pruned, abolishing such schemes would take away considerable Central government support to many states. From 2015, funding for many such programmes has been curtailed drastically, as substantial funds are now being transferred to the states under the Fourteenth Finance Commission award. Unfortunately, it has reduced the Centre's ability to support interventions in many areas of the states, especially health, and nutrition to children, education and rural development, where there are critical needs.

There was an interesting system prevalent at that time for the approval of plan sizes of states. Every year, sometime in the month of March–April, CMs of different states would come to the Planning Commission and discuss the plan size of the state with the deputy chairman and its members. Generally, there would be a discussion between the concerned member of the commission and the chief secretary of the state and his team, before the plan size of the state was discussed. Prior to this, members of the commission would often visit the state to assess development needs. For most of the states, this would be an occasion to project developments in the state, innovative schemes launched by them, the growth rate of the State Domestic Product (SDP), and financial resources and support required from the Central government. Generally, states were given some additional resource by the Deputy Chairman from his discretionary funds. In the commission there was a block grant for this purpose. One state that made a video presentation was Gujarat. PM Modi, then the CM of the state, however, did not like the members of the commission visiting states to hear complaints from NGOs, referred to as 'sunwai'. During this process, members of the public would usually complain against the administration, including state policies. He seemed especially upset when Syeda Saiyidain Hameed, a member of the commission, visited Gujarat. He raised this during our annual plan discussion and voiced his disapproval. Except for special-category states and J&K, other states got very little funds from the deputy chairman's discretionary grant. Still, almost all CMs visited the commission for these discussions.

Mayawati, then the CM of UP, was an exception. She did not come to any of the meetings of the Planning Commission for finalizing the plan of the state, which I was responsible for.

Usually, the plan sizes suggested by the states got approved. In case of Northeastern states and J&K, however, the plan was determined primarily by additional assistance given by the Planning Commission. This was a tough job. CMs wanted a large plan size, and considered it a political victory for them. I especially recall a closed-door meeting with the CMs of Manipur and Nagaland with the deputy chairman. They were so upset at not getting a commitment on the additional funds they wanted as special assistance from the Planning Commission that they just walked out. We could settle the issue only after several rounds of informal discussions.

The annual visits of the CMs and their teams gave us an excellent view of how the states were planning to grow, new initiatives by them, how successful their schemes were and the opportunity for the commission to share the experience with other states. Though the commission provided a good support system for many states when they put forward their problems with other ministries, I felt the system needed reforms.

The PM decided at that time to constitute an expert group to suggest measures required to accelerate UP's economic growth. I was asked to chair it. We used the Giri Institute of Development Studies (GIDS) in Lucknow to help us out. The committee had a good mix of economists and members of the business industry, apart from civil servants and representatives of the state government. I found it strange that the state government had little interest in my report finalized in October 2008. The government had not sponsored it and hence felt no need to work on it. Development had become a victim of politics in the state. The Lok Sabha elections were due a few months later, in April–May 2009. The ruling political party had no intention of letting the Centre get to the forefront of UP development. It was a question of development initiative to be taken advantage of later for political gains.

Integrating Northeastern States

The development of the Northeastern region has always been seriously hampered due to poor infrastructure and connectivity with other states of the country. Before 1947, the region was well connected with the rest of India via Bengal. After the Partition and separation of East Bengal, there was only a small corridor of about 25 km near Siliguri that connected the region with the rest of the country. We had very few flights going to Guwahati then, the gateway to the region; there were no regional airlines either. Road connectivity was a mess and rail connections did not touch some states. The region did not have good universities, and economic growth was slow. Power development in the region was poor and insurgency high.

Things, however, gradually began changing as development initiatives intensified. In the Planning Commission, we had certain funds available at the discretion of the deputy chairman. Traditionally, nearly half of these were used for providing additional resources to the Northeastern states. As the plan size got bigger and more funds were available, these were provided for new development projects. The full benefits of the funds provided to the Northeast did not reach the people earlier and there was a lot of leakage.

We instituted a system of third-party verification of projects. This revealed huge problems and massive leakage of funds. Schools had been built but at times only one wall had been completed; roads were only half completed. The new system corrected a number of these shortcomings.

There were a number of policy interventions made by the Central government, with strong support from the Planning Commission. This helped fill up many developmental gaps in the region. It was decided to have central universities in all states. All state capitals were to be connected by air and rail. A number of landing strips were identified, where smaller aircraft could land. A special project for the development of roads in the region was taken up. Funds for all of this were provided by the Central government ministries. The region had huge potential for hydel-power generation. But evacuation of power was tricky, as the land strip, referred to as the chicken's neck, through which these very high-voltage lines were to connect the region with the rest of India, was very narrow. Setting up towers of high voltage was also difficult in view of the competing usage of this strip of land. This was taken up in phases.

An important policy initiative to expand economic activity in the region was opening up contacts and border trade with the neighbouring countries of Myanmar, China and Bangladesh. Under the Look East policy, contact with other nations of South East Asia, including Thailand, was sought to be promoted.

Development of infrastructure in the region, however, threw up many challenges. Surprisingly, it was tough to acquire land in a region where the population density was so low. I recall the difficult time we had building the airport at Gangtok, the capital of Sikkim. The site of the airport was a little distance away from the town.

After most of the work for building the airport was completed, a number of families staked their claim to compensation. This took a lot of time to resolve, as AAI, which was building the airport, did not find any justification in spending this money. The problem was compounded by the fact that the airport was not considered financially viable by them. A similar difficulty arose when building an airport in Kohima, the capital of Nagaland. The problems were much more severe in the case of roads. But the building of these roads and bridges, and the rapid expansion of air connectivity and railway lines gave me enormous satisfaction. The Northeast was being brought closer to the rest of India.

I got an intimate feel of it when I travelled on the first test journey of the train to Naharlagun, a station next to Itanagar, the capital of Arunachal Pradesh, hitherto unconnected by rail. I had earlier argued in a meeting called by the PM for the allotment of additional funds to the railways for the completion of work in both segments: north of the Brahmaputra river to connect Arunachal Pradesh and south of it to convert narrow-gauge lines to broad-gauge, and work on the railway-line connectivity to Imphal, the capital of Manipur. This had been finally agreed to. Later, I could enthuse the railway officers to complete the work in time. This was the first time people in the area had seen the train, and they felt very excited. They wanted to know when a Rajdhani would start from Naharlagun. Later, a regular passenger service was started from this faraway region.

I focused on changing the agenda of discourse in the region. All meetings with public representatives were focused on this. The pace of development in the region was earlier slower than the national average. Many of these projects helped lift this up, and growth rates accelerated. This brought it closer to, and in some cases higher than, the national average.

◆

After joining the Planning Commission in June, I decided to visit Assam and Meghalaya for a quick assessment of the development programmes. While the region had eight states including Sikkim, nearly two-third of the population was in Assam alone. The state was a gateway to the entire region, with Guwahati as the hub. River Brahmaputra, which flows through the state, causes enormous damage and land erosion during floods. It was, therefore, crucial to assess the nature of the problems. Montek had also decided to join in. It was an extensive discussion and we identified gaps in the infrastructure that needed investment and measures that could increase the low agricultural productivity. In areas where there was a good paddy crop, there was no way to procure and provide remunerative prices to the farmers. It was clear that the state needed substantial investment. Several measures were supported by us to stimulate growth in the state. And infrastructural development was key to that. As part of the Assam Accord, it had been decided to set up a plant for cracking of gas to produce petrochemicals. This had been delayed and was resolved later, when GAIL was encouraged to take over the construction and complete the work. In upper Assam, the bridge across the Brahmaputra needed to be completed; the state needed to develop power capacities, as it had severe shortage; it simultaneously needed to strengthen the network of transmission lines; it needed to improve its education and health parameters; and air connectivity to Guwahati needed to be strengthened—we needed many more flights. I supported funds and policy interventions for expanding infrastructure in power, roads and flight connectivity to Guwahati. Things have vastly improved over the years. There has been a sharp increase in flights to Guwahati and huge investment has been made to expand the power network. The Guwahati airport has been modernized. These investments in development infrastructure have helped change things.

My first visit as member to Meghalaya was on a day when there was heavy downpour in the region. Shillong, the capital of the state, was also the headquarters of the North Eastern Council. It was connected to Guwahati with just a two-lane road. As I travelled from the Guwahati airport to Shillong, I felt that the condition of the road was terrible in several stretches. At places, I could not even see the road, as there was so much water on it. The road was winding, as hill roads usually are, and one was not sure when the next turn would make us plummet into a gorge deep in the mountains.

I reached Raj Bhawan, the residence of the governor, where I was staying; all officers had assembled for a meeting there. We discussed the development issues. Over the next seven years, I visited the state a number of times and saw the development strategy unfold. The road between Guwahati and Shillong is now four-lane; there has been development of horticulture and floriculture; the airport at Shillong is being expanded; and the state has developed hydel-power potential. An interesting aside is, however, about Cherrapunji, which is about a two-hour drive from Shillong. This hill town was once said to receive the highest rainfall in the world. It seems that forests were intact those days. Even now, it receives fairly heavy rain but the slopes have been denuded. Villages around it have a huge shortage of drinking water and the hills have lost all soil cover. Cherrapunji is now a rain desert. When the first schemes for its revival were prepared—and the Planning Commission was keen to support this initiative—Israel suggested that nearly 80 per cent of the fund be used for the import of special containers from Israel, which would store drinking water for different villages! Only a small amount was kept for revival of soil cover. We rejected the idea and the state prepared a fresh approach, focusing on the revival of soil cover. This was the right decision, as I saw the result on the hill slopes of Cherrapunji in subsequent years.

One morning, as I was settling down for work in the commission, Dorjee Khandu, the then CM of Arunachal Pradesh, came to meet me. He was concerned about the infrastructure of the state, which was in terrible condition. He brought a report with him indicating the list of half-completed roads, incomplete bridges, unelectrified villages and the scanty water supply to Itanagar town. As a border state with sensitive regions around, it needed special support. I decided to send a team to the state to take a look at the gaps in infrastructure and assess its financial needs. This was done quickly, and we were able to allocate funds to the state for the completion of several projects when the PM announced a special financial support and development package for the state.

Later, when I flew to the area and met the villagers along the Chinese border, I realized the aspirations of the people there. In villages across the border, in China, investments had been made in electrification and housing. But in many of our villages along the Chinese border, there was still no electricity, and transmission lines for power were far away. We decided to provide electricity by using non-conventional energy sources. There were a number of streams running through the terrain. These were very useful in generating electricity. Solar power was the other way out, though it was exorbitant in those days. The most difficult part, however, was fixing the road infrastructure. In many cases, the villagers had to travel for at least a few days to reach the state headquarters. Making foodgrains available under the public distribution system was a challenge. This needed reform.

Khandu accompanied me on one of my visits and insisted that I see the progress made in some of the otherwise inaccessible areas. I visited a school and had an excellent interaction with the children there. I felt great pleasure seeing the schools and the children studying there. But when I asked them how far they travelled to reach their school, it was the CM who took me out of the room and showed me a deep gorge, saying that half of the students came from a village across it, just 1 km away. In the rains, however, they did not come to school at all.

The CM suggested that I evaluate the development work in the Tawang area. He hailed from the region and was keen that it be provided financial support. We first flew in his helicopter and then drove to the guest house located another 500 metres higher. It was very cold. When I went to my room, I found that efforts had been made to heat it up. But I was still shivering. After some time, Khandu turned up with special woollen clothing. 'Please put these on if you want to be comfortable,' he remarked. He advised me to rest for some time to acclimatize myself to the lower oxygen level in the air.

As he took me around the next day, he explained that everyone in the area understood Hindi and spoke it fluently. He was, in fact, very proud of it. During the course of this tour, I visited

Tawang Monastery, which was a great spiritual experience. It was interesting to see the studies being done by the monks there. They were keen to spread the message of Buddhism, but were short of funds. We were able to provide some financial assistance to the state later for the development of the infrastructure at the monastery.

However, the issue that still plagues the state is that despite having half of the country's hydel-power potential, Arunachal Pradesh has not been able to use it in the absence of road infrastructure and problems with Assam. This needs early resolution.

◆

Economic activities and infrastructure in most Northeastern states picked up, and Sikkim continued to record the highest rate of growth among these. I had visited the state briefly sometime in 2005 as Cabinet secretary and met the CM, Pawan Chamling. He appeared quiet but effective. My first impression was later confirmed when I visited the state subsequently and looked at its development strategy. The state has effectively used its hydel-power potential and developed floriculture, especially tulips, and tourism along with it. Later, as a strategy, the government decided to promote organic farming and develop the state entirely on those lines. The effort was supported by us with resources and policy interventions. During my visits and discussions with the state, it was clear that the biggest problem the state faced was difficulty in reaching the state boundries via neighbouring West Bengal. The road that passed through West Bengal and connected to Gangtok was invariably either closed due to Gorkhaland agitation or extremely crowded due to traffic and expansion work.

The journey to Gangtok was, therefore, always troublesome for tourists. While an airport was developed near Gangtok, it took a while and could provide only limited passenger access. A rail link is now being built. In spite of these limitations, the per capita income of the state is the highest in the region.

◆

Nagaland is different from all the other states of the Northeast. It was created as a separate state by an Act of Parliament and, in 1963, had its first Assembly election. Unfortunately, insurgency has affected the state. The government had appointed interlocutors to negotiate a settlement with the two main insurgent groups— Nationalist Socialist Council of Nagalim (Isak-Muivah), or NSCN-(IM), and National Socialist Council of Nagaland-Khaplang, or NSCN-K. Talks were on for quite some time. In between, there was relative peace. But I was aware that the insurgent groups were still collecting a 'tax'. (An accord has been reached with Naga groups recently. Details of this are, however, not in the public domain.)

During my visit to the state, I was conscious of Nagas' political aspirations and insurgent activity. But gradually, I found that development efforts were having a good impact. More funds were, however, needed for the expansion of the road network, and the education and health sectors. The state had developed horticulture; it was expanding bamboo plantation, and papermaking units were needed to fully utilize it. They wanted to use bamboo in all other forms for micro and small enterprises. It has now developed some units. The state also has petroleum resources. Unfortunately, an agreement with the Central government on its extraction has been difficult. Both are claiming ownership of the resource. Given that the resource may not be large, the Central government should give a special dispensation and permit Nagaland to exploit and use this as they wish.

During our annual discussion on plans, or possibly later, I received a memorandum through post that enough funds were not being passed on to eastern Nagaland and that the area was being ignored. I sent a message to the state government that I wanted to visit the easternmost part of Nagaland, bordering Myanmar, on my next tour of the state. On reaching the district, I found tremendous enthusiasm among residents. In the meeting held there, people talked of separate funding for the area. I could see that the district lacked infrastructure and that people were comparatively not so well off. The DM handled it well. I also met the chief of the tribe, who was a warrior, and accompanied by the DM and the police escort, I landed at his place. The area was a collection of huts, and I saw some human heads (perhaps war trophies) hanging in many places. The chief and a few other people met me and gave a representation, and invited me to look around the complex. As I entered the chief's hut, a very old lady, probably around 80 years old, walked past me. I was told that the tribal chief had many concubines and that she was one of them. I was presented with a garland of human heads. Mercifully, these were of metal. When I landed back in Kohima, the CM was waiting for me. He and some of his ministers explained that there was no discrimination against the eastern region and that funds were being fairly distributed. I, however, saw a clear need for larger devolution of resources to the region.

◆

Tripura was, again, different from the other Northeastern states in many ways. Politically, it had a Left government for nearly a quarter of a century. The CM Manik Sarkar was in office since 1998. He was a simple and unassuming man, with very little ostentation in official functions. The state had, in 2008–09, almost done away with insurgency. With our financial support, it was able to build a new Assembly and other administrative infrastructure in its capital, Agartala, in the next five years. It used its own funds and special grants given by the Planning Commission efficiently to improve the productivity of paddy and undertake rubber plantation. This helped improve the income of the common man and provide employment. The biggest problem the state faced, however, was inaccessibility and poor connectivity with mainland India. I was conscious of this and, at every opportunity, supported its initiatives to improve infrastructure: widen roads, convert narrow-gauge railway lines to broad-gauge, and implement other policy measures.

ONGC had earlier discovered natural gas reserves in the state. This was used to set up a gas-based power plant by ONGC. I recall the difficulty in transporting the gas turbines for the power plant. These were heavy, and the roads, especially the bridges, could not take their weight. It was, therefore, decided to transport the turbines via waterways through Bangladesh. By this route, the distance was shorter and it was possible to bring the heavy turbines to the site of the plant. The operation was a success. It provided sufficient power to Tripura and other states of the region. However, the CM was keen that some power be shared with Bangladesh to soften them and make them agree to improve connectivity. This would bring the Chittagong port within easy reach of the state. Later, the state government strongly supported the international agreements with

Bangladesh, which was signed by the Government of India. These provided for 100 MW power from the Tripura power plant, easy access to India from the Chittagong port and exchange of enclaves, apart from other areas of cooperation.

◆

Economic activity and development had interesting implications for insurgency in Manipur. After the intervention of CM Okram Ibobi Singh with the MHA, I remember the government had agreed to vacate the Kangla Fort, then being used by the Assam Rifles, and make it available for civilian use. This was an emotional issue for the local population. When I visited Manipur for the first time in 2008, I had strong police protection, supported by CRPF jawans. Four years down the line, when I visited Loktak lake—which was earlier infested with insurgents—work on cleaning the lake and providing jobs to fishermen were both on in full swing. There was also no extra protection and the officer at the CRPF post near the lake was enjoying the sight of his lovely surroundings. Roads, too, were under construction. Funds from the Planning Commission were also used to set up the new high court building in Manipur and a special women's market. It helped develop infrastructure in districts, including the setting up of hospitals. One of the biggest hospitals was developed near Imphal with these funds.

◆

The population of Mizoram is almost entirely Christian; and the church had a lot of influence during election time. The incomes of the people were low, and except for paddy and bamboo, there was little agriculture. Industry, too, was minimal. But literacy levels were one of the highest in the country. The region had been buffeted with insurgency until the 1980s, when the then Prime Minister Rajiv Gandhi settled the issue with the Mizoram Accord, 1986, and brought the Mizoram National Front (MNF) under mainstream Indian democracy. CM Zoramthanga was very informal in his attitude and often stopped by my room for discussions on development issues and financial support. He was keen that I be appointed governor of Mizoram and I learnt informally that he had written a letter to the PM about it. Perhaps this reflected his uneasy relation with the Governor, Amolak Rattan Kohli. Later, when Lal Thanhawla became the CM, we tried to develop alternative vocations that could fetch the people better incomes. Gradually, we were able to promote grape cultivation. When it was only in a small area, there was no problem related to the market. As it expanded, a winery had to be set up to process the grapes and produce wine. This was where the conflict arose. The church was not in favour of wine, as it considered alcohol harmful for the population. Finally, economic argument won and Lal Thanhawla was able to persuade the church. (Recently the MNF won the election, and Zorma Thanga, after taking over as the CM, introduced prohibition. It is not clear how they will handle grape production.) I recall how, when I was staying with the Governor, he served Mizo wine at dinner with great pride and presented a bottle to me as a gift from the Mizo people. Later, we also provided financial resources for a special programme for the development of all families, weaning them from 'jhuming' (shifting) cultivation and giving them the option to develop alternative vocations.

Diversity Is the Differentiator: The Thirteenth Finance Commission

The government decided to constitute the Thirteenth Finance Commission under the chairmanship of Vijay Kelkar, sometime in November 2007, a few months after I joined the Planning Commission. I was appointed by the PM as a member of the Finance Commission, a body provided under the Constitution to recommend the sharing of tax revenues of the Central government with the states. In addition, it also made recommendations on transfers to each state in accordance with its special needs. We were expected to give our recommendations by December 2009, and these were to be implemented from April 2010 for a period of five years. While technically we made recommendations to the President of India, in actual practice, these had always been accepted as a matter of tradition by the government. This cast an extra responsibility on the Finance Commission while making its recommendations.

Over the next two years, my time was divided between the two bodies—the Finance Commission and the Planning Commission. The Finance Commission carried out many studies to firm up its ideas and visited all the states to get the views of the CMs and other institutions involved in the development of the states. It interacted with Central departments and the Planning Commission to know their viewpoints as well. By way of consultation, it tried to reach all sections. Like all other previous commissions, it faced several difficult questions.

Assessment of revenues to be given to the states depended primarily upon the expenditure projected by the states over the next five years. We also had to keep in mind the needs of the

Central government for defence, maintenance and plan expenditure. A large devolution to states would mean reduced Centrally sponsored schemes on health, education, employment, rural development, drinking water and electrification. While the Finance Commission was opposed to so many Centrally sponsored schemes, the Planning Commission held an opposite view. I had a tough time balancing these two opposite viewpoints. Much later, commenting on this dilemma, Y.V. Reddy, chairman of the Fourteenth Finance Commission, with whom the Planning Commission was having discussions on its approach, jocularly remarked, 'You had to stand where you sat.'

A visit to the states and seeing the working of panchayats and village development at the grass-roots level is a very humbling experience. India has varied problems that differ in nature and intensity as you travel from Arunachal Pradesh to Ladakh, the border areas of Himachal Pradesh, the plains of UP and the coastal areas of Goa. They present different dimensions of the problem of governance and economic growth. During my travels across the country, I found some individuals extremely impressive in their interaction with us. Tarun Gogoi, the then CM of Assam, was one of them. He was an old-timer and it was his second term as CM. During his hour-long speech before the Finance Commission, he did not look at any paper. He highlighted the problems of the state, gave statistics that were broadly acceptable and talked of challenges to growth and his need for resources. As we questioned him, he did not falter even once.

Another interesting and powerful presentation came in 2008–09 from Parkash Singh Badal, the then CM of Punjab. He was already 80 years old at that time, but spoke powerfully, without much support of any paper, and highlighted the special problems of the border state, especially of farmers and their families staying near the international border. He highlighted how the water table in many districts of the state had gone down drastically and posed a huge threat to farmers. And later, at lunch, in his inimitable style, he regaled us with stories of politicians.

The visit to Gujarat added a different dimension to my travels. The state was doing well, and such states were generally not keen on meeting the Finance Commission. The difficulty was that while distributing the share of taxes earmarked for the states by the commission, strong weightage was given to states with low per capita incomes. Well-off states such as Gujarat were unhappy that they did not get resources in proportion to their population. Modi gave a very good opening speech, in which he highlighted the achievements of Gujarat in agriculture, and diversification to floriculture, which was bringing in good incomes for farmers.

An officer of the state recalled that during the CM's review of the power sector, on finding the poor rate of village electrification, he suggested a change of strategy. He advised two separate power-transmission lines from the nearby power substation: one for residential use with small transformers and the other for agricultural use. This was a great success.

While the economic indicators were good, the commission noticed that social indicators of the state were not commensurate with the high per capita incomes. The indicators were not good in either education or health. The number of girls per thousand boys was below the national average. Our colleague and eminent economist Indira Rajaraman spoke powerfully on this issue. Modi assured us that this imbalance was indeed uppermost on his mind and that he had launched schemes that would surely improve the situation. However, Gujarat faces the problem of bad social indicators even today. After 2014, according to the CAG report, the maternal mortality rate has deteriorated, though the neonatal mortality rate is better. The literacy rate is lower than that of neighbouring Maharashtra.

In the final report of the Finance Commission, we increased the share of states in Central taxes by 2.5 per cent over the previous commission's. It was not a huge jump but consistent with the approach that the Finance Commissions had to take special care of the states' interests. While we were finalizing the report, it was clear to me that several states were going to be unhappy. In our quest for a fair and transparent distribution of the kitty among the states, we had devised a formula that had broadly given weightage to population, per capita incomes and how much less they were than the highest per capita-income state of the country, the area of the state and its efforts in raising taxes commensurate with its capacity.

Even after providing for special weightage to some states, there were financial resource gaps. The CM of Tripura was the most unhappy with me; Himachal Pradesh was similarly dissatisfied. The difficulty was that these two states had a very high expenditure on employees. Considering their populations, they had far more employees than other states. The commission had fixed a norm beyond which it did not consider staff reasonable and did not provide for it in its financial projections. The two states, however, were soft on this issue and did not want any reduction in the strength of their employees. This led to a shortage of resources for development activities. Except Assam, none of the Northeastern states found the

Finance Commission award adequate for their needs. Much later, we provided grants from the Planning Commission to meet this gap. In fact, Pranab Mukherjee, then the finance minister, had a special meeting of all CMs of the Northeastern states to assure them of Central support.

The problem of these states is lack of an adequate tax base. They are heavily dependent on grants from the Central government through different windows. Imposition of normative behaviour has not worked. The recent award of the Fourteenth Finance Commission has increased the share of all states in taxes, especially those with large forest areas. However, the total flow of funds to them may not increase sharply, as financial resources earlier available under the plan may not be available still.

Catalysing Investments in Infrastructure

The PM was conscious of the need for investment in infrastructure. He wanted to look at the performance of the sector closely and evaluate the measures required to resolve the bottlenecks. I undertook this task in the Planning Commission. Every month, I would look at the power, rail, road, port and airport sectors, and send him my assessment. Often, I would call on him and give him a personal briefing about these areas. These were occasions to discuss other issues as well. He was keen to know our assessment of how the states, especially those in the Northeast, were progressing. During these meetings, many issues emerged that required policy changes. I was keen to get a resolution for several of these. It had become clear that government funding was not adequate to step up the pace of construction in most of these sectors—public-private partnership (PPP) was essential to move it forward.

This was happening in other countries as well. But we required it on a large scale.

The concept of PPP had already been mentioned in the Eleventh Plan and was projected as a key source of infrastructure-funding. Construction of power plants and power-transmission lines had excellent potential. In fact, since the 1990s, the sector had been opened for participation by private players. They could own power plants and provide power to distribution companies. However, response to this policy had been poor. One of the reasons was that Bharat Heavy Electricals Limited (BHEL) was the sole manufacturer of power plants and it had a small capacity, which was fully booked. Now the Chinese power-plant manufacturers decided to offer their services and equipment. China had huge surplus manufacturing capacity of power plants. There were a few other companies too. An important bottleneck was thus removed. The domestic production of coal was expanding as well. The prices were attractive for the manufacturers, as against imported coal.

The states were keen to set up new power plants so that the chronic shortage of power, a major cause of slow industrial and commercial growth, could be removed. An important addition to demand for power was the rapid increase in rural electrification. A scheme called Rajiv Gandhi Grameen Vidyutikaran Yojana (RGGVY) had been launched for universal electrification. Per capita incomes were already rising, with a high and sustained GDP growth. This led to new demands for power from the expanding domestic network and widespread use of electrical appliances, especially of television. Domestic demand for power increased rapidly. This led to an almost triple upturn in private investment in power generation and a quantum jump in the addition of new power plants to provide electricity.

The telecom sector also expanded rapidly during this period. Demand for communication was growing, and with the low rates of mobile-phone calls and talk-time charges, and growing rural incomes, the number of connections expanded rapidly. From about 6 crore connections in March 2003, the number increased to 95 crore by March 2012. Large investments took place in the mobile telecom infrastructure to support this expansion, primarily by private players.

Several private investments were done in PPP mode. Of these, the most interesting was the road sector. Earlier, the NHAI had taken up construction of the Golden Quadrilateral, which connected Delhi, Mumbai, Chennai and Kolkata. This had been done by funds generated from the cess on petrol and diesel available with the government. It was now planned that a number of new roads would be constructed and maintained by private players. The roads were to be tolled, and the revenues thus generated were to be collected by a private player (called concessionaire). The concessionaire was allowed to collect toll for about fifteen to twenty years at agreed rates. Studies were undertaken to assess the traffic of cars, buses and other vehicles expected to use that road. This would determine the expected revenue from the toll. Part of the cost of the road was also to be provided by the government as subsidy, which was termed 'viability gap funding'. While the concessionaire thus provided funds for road construction, it recovered its investment and profit on it from the toll revenue and the government subsidy. The concessionaire was chosen from among those who bid in an open tender and asked for minimum viability gap funding from the government. If heavy traffic was expected on the new road, the private players would at times offer grants to the government. In such cases, the selection was made based on the grants offered by the concessionaire. This model was adopted by the NHAI and a number of state governments to expand the network of roads quite successfully.

Apart from roads, private funding was undertaken in the PPP mode for the Delhi and Mumbai airport expansion and modernization. But most of the modernization of other airports was done by the AAI from its own resources. The modernization and expansion of ports was undertaken both in PPP mode and through private investment. This led to a large expansion in capacities as demand for traffic grew.

As projects were taken on for implementation under the PPP mode, the decision whether to do so in annuity mode or toll mode was critical. Under the annuity mode, a private investor would build the road from his funds and borrowing from the market, and the government would pay him in instalments over an agreed period. The Planning Commission was strongly opposed to the annuity method. There were questions related to the project costs. This was a key factor for determining the viability gap funding or the subsidy to be made available to the private player building the road. There were several issues to be resolved on the terms of the concession agreement as well. Many private players wanted an early exit from the project by transferring their responsibility for maintenance of the road over the next fifteen years or so to another player. There was also the question of the need to introduce a clause on mid-term negotiation on concession terms with any change in the economic environment, as project viability could be affected. There were other questions related to project design, delays in environment clearance, and land acquisition and its financial implication on the project. There was also the issue of resolving the financial claims of private players. These were large amounts and a transparent, commercially viable mechanism had to be put in place to set this right.

I chaired a number of committees, which suggested specific policy decisions to resolve several of these issues. In August 2009, I sent a report suggesting several changes in the terms of awarding of a contract for the road sector. The issue of PPP, however, led to some strong interdepartmental turf wars. In the Planning Commission, we had a competent strong-willed senior civil servant who had done a lot of work in this area. He suggested model concession agreements in different infrastructural areas. The Planning Commission stood by it. But the Ministry of Finance thought this area was its remit and had already issued guidelines on these issues, especially the viability gap funding and its modalities. The ministries would often appoint a consultant who had their own ideas. While this was the period in which private investment boomed, it was also the period in which interministerial differences slowed down progress. With a lot of private investment flowing in, inevitably there was talk of corruption.

Sadly, private investments spur growth but also attract political and bureaucratic corruption in economies such as India.

Policymaking: Resolving Complex Issues

Work in the Planning Commission also involved extensive participation in policymaking. Practically all proposals were referred to the commission for advice. This was normally given by the planning secretary with the approval of the deputy chairman.

Members were generally involved in a few selected cases in which there were several alternatives and the commission needed a closer look. Often, ministers would request members of the commission to chair committees to suggest policy in areas that needed extensive consultations. At times, the PM would constitute a committee to consider evolving a public policy in certain sectors. I had one of the largest number of such committees with me.* Three committees whose reports had wide-ranging implications included those on oil prices, Centrally sponsored schemes and hydel-power projects on the Ganga.

The year 2008 saw one of the sharpest rises in crude oil prices. The prices rose continuously from the annual average price of $64.2 in 2007 to $91.2 in 2008. On 11 July, the prices hit $147 per barrel, which had a direct impact on the prices of petrol, diesel and LPG. This sharp rise would have hit the middle class and the poor very badly if the entire price burden were to be passed on to consumers. But it could not be left to the oil companies by themselves—prices had to be increased. The PM asked me to chair a committee of experts, which included two eminent economists, the late Saumitra Chaudhuri and Arvind Virmani. We were clear that price increase had to take place to reflect the sharp jump in crude prices. After looking at the balance sheets and costing of the processing and marketing network of oil companies, we suggested a sharing of the financial burden by oil companies, the ONGC (which was to provide crude from domestic production), the government (in the form of financial support) and consumers

---

*A list at the end of this chapter will give readers an idea of how the Planning Commission played a critical role in governance during the period (2007–2014).

(in the form of a hike in the prices of petrol, etc). However, we also indicated a gradual increase in prices to let the market adjust to this. Our report was promptly rejected by the oil ministry, which was looking for a solution that involved zero price rise for consumers. This was absurd. Much later, the report was dusted and implemented in 2013, when oil prices were high again and the government had to tighten its belt on financial resources.

An important area of policymaking that I handled was the problem of proliferation of Centrally sponsored schemes. Since Independence, the Central government had been acutely aware that the states were short of resources and, in pursuing populist policies, did not invest enough in certain sectors important for national growth. The government decided to launch schemes under which states got funds for certain schematic expenditures like education and health. The Constitution provides for certain subjects to be within the purview of the state government and others to be handled by the Central government. Some subjects are part of the concurrent list of the Constitution. Over the years, in successive plans, the Central government has kept on making schemes in areas such as agriculture, irrigation, education, health, power, drinking water and land development that are either state subjects or within the competence of both. The number of such schemes proliferated in successive plans. In every meeting of the NDC, CMs made powerful pleas to reduce the number of such schemes. Considering the seriousness of this problem, a number of committees were set up in different meetings of the NDC. Unfortunately, most of the suggestions that emerged were of marginal nature and even these were not implemented. There was no will in the commission to give up its turf.

So when a committee was formed under me to resolve the issue, I had to work with the ministries and get a broad consensus from them. Very soon I realized that the best way was to interact with all the concerned departments of the Central government and make them agree on reducing the number of schemes. Since it was highly unlikely that they would agree on cutting down their financial allocation, I decided to ask them to reduce the schemes within the same overall financial allocation. This provided flexibility to the states to spend in any sector, and even use larger amounts for a problem specific to that state. I also suggested a flexi-grant, which could be used in any area decided by the state. We tried this out in every ministry. Many times the secretaries got upset, but having been a Cabinet secretary proved to be an advantage.

Finally, I reduced the schemes to about 60 from more than 170. I also made recommendations against future proliferation and put safeguards in place. After my report on Centrally sponsored schemes was sent to the states for their comments, there was huge support from them, with practically every state government pleading for its implementation. In the meeting of the NDC, which was held after the states had got the report, several CMs requested for its early implementation. Later, several suggestions were accepted and got incorporated in the budget. With the change in government in 2014, abolition of the Planning Commission and the setting up of NITI Aayog (also known as the National Institution for Transforming India), another exercise was undertaken, as the Fourteenth Finance Commission had substantially increased the state's share of taxes of the Central government from 32.5 per cent to 42.5 per cent, and many schemes needed to be funded by the states. I was, however, happy that our report on Centrally sponsored schemes had suggested a path that had been broadly accepted and led to an important reform in our governance structure.

Yet another contentious area was the question of setting up hydel-power plants on River Ganga and its tributaries in the hills of Uttarakhand. The committee, apart from various ministries and the state government of Uttarakhand, included several experts and non-official representatives, such as Sunita Narain, the director general of the Centre for Science and Environment (CSE); the director of Indian Institute of Technology, Roorkee; the chairman of Central Electricity Authority (CEA); and the chairman of the Central Water Commission. There were initially two major concerns: whether any more hydel-power plants should be allowed on the river and the environmental safeguards needed for the current and the new plants. During the course of the committee's work, another issue related to the Dhari Devi temple in the state was referred to it. Several people from the area had represented to the government that the temple was in danger of being flooded, as the Srinagar power project was under construction. This was a hydel-power project involving the construction of a dam on the Alaknanda river. Since the temple was in an area that would get submerged once the dam was filled, several representations were made by different groups requesting that the construction be halted. The company constructing the dam presented before the committee a plan under which the idols would be lifted and put on a platform built higher but at the same place where the temple was now. There was also an alternative plan of building a well around the temple. The construction company also suggested how the new temple could be safer and consistent with the people's needs. A group of residents from the area were, however, opposed to it. As rains intensified in the area, it was clear that unless the temple idols were lifted, these would get submerged. An expert committee consisting of the chairmen of the CEA and the Central Water Commission was rushed to the spot. They came back with a report that the only option to save the temple was to lift the idols and instal them higher in the new temple being built. There was intense lobbying on this issue. We, however, sent our recommendations to the environment ministry based on expert advice.

Meanwhile, we continued our work on assessing the potential for setting up hydel-power plants on the Ganga and its tributaries upstream of Haridwar. There was strong public sentiment against such construction, as it was argued that many below 5 MW power plants permitted by the state government had polluted the environment and ecology. Large areas on the riverbed had apparently completely dried up due to these power plants. Public sentiment was so strong that a group of persons sat on a day-long dharna outside the Yojna Bhawan, where Planning Commission was located, and demanded to see me while I was discussing ramifications of the alternatives with my colleagues. I met them at the dharna site. They were opposed to the setting up of any power plant on the Ganga or its tributaries, and gave a representation, which was duly taken note of. At that time, the hydel-power capacity of the river had been utilized to the extent of only one-fourth of its potential, as assessed by the CEA. We had a strong representation from the state government of Uttarakhand, which wanted very few restrictions and relaxed environmental norms on the power plants proposed. They argued that there was limited economic potential in the state and if power was available cheaply, industry could develop and provide new employment opportunities. Religious leaders, on the other hand, felt that the riverbed should not be interfered with and that separate channels should be constructed for power plants, if at all. Environmentalists were also opposed to the power plants and argued that the construction of new power plants would lead to a lot of debris being thrown into the streams and near the riverbeds, which would quickly find its way into the river. They felt that damage to greenery and ecology was quite large and identified biodiversity in the river that needed to be preserved; NGOs, too, wanted a continuous flow of water in the river and were opposed to run-of-river plants, which left large sections of the riverbed dry. We had extensive discussions in our committee both formally and informally on the issue. I was quite clear in my mind that biodiversity had to be protected. Certain areas that were so far quite clean and had little potential for hydel power had to be saved too. It was also necessary to ensure that there would be water in the riverbed throughout the year to meet local needs. But I was also not willing to accept the argument that the people of the area should be deprived of their hydel-power potential, which was a key economic factor for their growth.

Narain visited the Kumbh Mela to take stock of the water pollution at Sangam, the confluence of the rivers Ganga and Yamuna. She also looked at the pollution levels slightly upstream and studied other measures such as the use of bio-remedial techniques on the nullahs flowing into the river to minimize pollution. This was in addition to the sewage treatment plant (STP) used to ensure that cleaner water flowed into the river. A number of open drains were interconnected to bring a larger volume of sewage and open drain water into the STP to be treated by it and then discharged into the river. This ensured better utilization of the STP capacity and far cleaner water flowing into the river. During the Kumbh, stricter controls were exercised on the discharge of polluted water or untreated sewage from upstream tanneries or other industrial units. The most important step was, of course, the release of a substantial volume of water into the river from the Ganga canal. A combination of these measures was used in the Kumbh to provide clean water for bathing and for other mela activities. I am convinced that the strategy should be adopted on a long-term basis to keep the Ganga clean.

We finally gave our report to the Ministry of Environment, Forest and Climate Change. We provided rather stiff environment norms and suggested the use of hydel-power potential of the river up to 60 per cent. There were comments and dissenting notes from two members, which were annexed. I was disappointed that I was not able to get a unanimous report. Interestingly, the SC looked at these issues and relied extensively on the report for a decision on the Dhari Devi temple issue. It, however, suggested that a technical committee be set up to look at other power plants. Interestingly, most of the individuals that the court identified for the evaluation of these power plants were already part of my committee. Also, the plants that the Wildlife Institute of India (WII) had discussed had already been looked at by us. Possibly, the court was not aware of these developments or did not examine them during the hearing. It only highlights how decisions get prolonged so often in our governance system.

Abolishing the Planning Commission: A Knee-Jerk Reaction?

The Planning Commission was abolished in 2014 after the new government took over and NITI Aayog was set up as its successor body. Earlier too, there had been a wide range of arguments against the planning body. There was a view that the commission was a remnant of the era when India had adopted a model of development inspired by the growth strategy in former USSR. However, since then, the country had opened up its economy and, after liberalization in the 1990s, private investment was largely driving the growth process. The organization had hence outlived its utility. It was also argued that the states needed to be empowered more and the Planning Commission allocating resources to them was not in conformity with the new economic realities. Some critics maintained that the Planning Commission was not in touch with ground realities. They cited the poverty line fixed by the commission as proof of it; NGOs felt it should be at a much higher income level. Finally, it was said that the commission in a modern era of liberalization was only an anachronism.

Despite these criticisms, I believe this decision was not very well thought out. It is clear that the Planning Commission needed reforms. It needed more professional expertise and a reduction in its strength. But we do need a body to develop a national vision and indicate broad directions and policies needed for economic growth. We require an institution that can evaluate the performance of schemes in different states and suggest corrective measures. In many areas, there are huge disparities among states. The per capita incomes are still in the ratio of 1:5 for the poorest states of the country as against the richest. Within the states, poorly developed areas, such as Bundelkhand in UP, the Kalahandi-Koraput and Balangir districts in Odisha, northern Karnataka and eastern Nagaland, apart from many others, need special support. Though the Finance Commission suggests resource allocation to states over a five-year period, we need a body to take care of evolving needs and development aspirations.

In a country with widely divergent levels of development and limited fiscal capacity in many states, we need an institution with resources to address the issues of infrastructural development in these areas to stimulate the development process. For example, the Northeastern states and J&K need continuous attention and financial resources. I remember how, during the annual plan discussions, the Northeast and J&K would suggest new financial resources. However, we would invariably be informed mid-year that they were falling short. In J&K, the realization of electricity dues was always a cause for serious concern, as it drained the resources of the state. Recovering even 50 per cent of the dues was a difficult task. There is also a great need for capacity-building in most of these states. They need support to prepare plans to access funds from Centrally sponsored schemes and to monitor their implementation. Many of these states cannot by themselves prepare plans and projects for exploiting their resource base. They need a planning body that can help them with both financial resources and the building of human resources.

There are wide disparities in the levels of health and education among states. We need to step up our expenditure in these sectors and plan for ensuring early implementation of Millennium Development Goals (MDGs). Nearly a hundred districts in the country need supportive developmental initiative to address the problem of left-wing extremism. These issues require a strategy, financial support from the Central government and a new set of policies.

NITI Aayog is a think tank with very little financial resources that it can provide to the states in dire need of funds. The states or the departments are not likely to interact with mere think tanks that don't have the ability to resolve their problems by giving financial support.

In 2012, I was invited in an advisory role by the newly established National Planning Commission of South Africa. We had extensive discussions on our models of development, infrastructural problems and implementation of plans. After the meeting, the chairman, who was a former finance minister, asked me whether the Planning Commission had any financial authority. I explained to him the system of plan outlays and the discretionary plan funds with the deputy chairman and how the commission had a major say in various policy issues. He explained to me his dilemma. The South African commission had prepared a fine plan and sent it to all the departments. But when the departments were asked about its implementation, they said they would respond in due course—and the plans just sat decorating their shelves. The commission was clearly adding little value to growth policies.

That NITI Aayog should be a think tank is a very unwise idea. It is likely to gradually become yet another government body preparing reports that will remain just documents, like so many other reports in various organizations.

LIST OF POLICY REPORTS

Sl.	Name of Report	Month/Year
1	High-Powered Committee on Financial Position of Oil Companies	July 2008
2	Study Group for Preparation of a Roadmap for Rapid Economic Development of Uttar Pradesh	October 2008
3	Revised Strategy for Implementation of National Highways Development Project, or NHDP (First Report)	August 2009
4	Committee on Faster Implementation of NHDP (Second Report)	February 2010
5	Committee on Port Sector	September 2010
6	Interministerial Task Force for Ceiling on Annuity Commitments	September 2010
7	High-Powered Review Committee on Various Aspects of the Agreement between Antrix and M/s Devas Multimedia Pvt Ltd	March 2011
8	Committee on Restructuring of Centrally Sponsored Schemes (CSS)	September 2011
9	Committee to Suggest Solutions on Coal and Other Development Issues	July 2012
10	Interministerial Task Force on Draft Port Regulatory Authority Bill	July 2012
11	Interministerial Task Force on Financing Plan for Airports	July 2012

12	Expert Group on Restructuring of Hindustan Aeronautics Limited (HAL)	September 2012
13	Committee to Suggest Solutions on Bid Conditions for Procurement of Super Critical Power Plants	February 2013
14	Interministerial Task Force on Issues Related to River Ganga and Interim Report on Dhari Devi Temple	September 2012/ April 2013
15	Interministerial Group to Identify Captive Projects in Sectors Other Than Power Sector and Assess Their Coal Requirement	November 2013
16	Committee to Study Development in Hill States Arising from Management of Forest Lands with Special Focus on Creation of Infrastructure, Livelihood and Human Development	November 2013
17	Interministerial Committee on Capital Dredging for Major Ports	December 2013
18	Creative Financing for Railways	April 2014
19	Committee on Restructuring of Debt of Discoms	2013

Chapter 7

UPA-II: AN OPPORTUNITY LOST

At the time of the formation of the UPA government in 2004, it did not have a majority in Parliament. It was only due to the outside support of the CPI(M), the SP and the BSP that the UPA was able to enjoy the majority parliamentary support in the Lok Sabha. In addition, it was a coalition of several political parties that had their own agendas. While some of the parties shared the CMP of the UPA, others had their own manifestos, which, in several ways, were different from the CMP. Also, investigations on charges of criminal misconduct were being conducted by the CBI against some leaders. It was in the interest of some of the parties to support the government. In view of its dependence on outside support, the government did not have a strong base. The most critical support for the UPA-I was from the CPI(M) and like-minded parties, which had nearly sixty MPs in the Lok Sabha. They exercised a strong influence due to their numbers. It was felt that they often flexed their political muscle to get their viewpoints accepted. But it was during the nuclear deal with the US that the government stood its ground and won a motion of confidence in the Lok Sabha in 2008.

In April–May 2009, the UPA came to power again and formed the government with the support of more than 320 members, including that of the BSP, the SP and a stronger showing on its own. The Indian economy had showed healthy growth in the earlier years. There were, however, several dark clouds on the horizon. After the failure of the Lehman Brothers, the global economy was in a crisis. The G8 had decided to provide stimulus for growth in the respective countries. India, too, was working on it and pumping money to sustain the level of growth and support global efforts aimed at preventing a recession. However, a more worrisome development was the sharp rise in the international prices of crude oil. The prices of energy were largely governed by this. From a low of $30 per barrel in 2004, it had touched $140 per barrel in 2008 and, in 2009, was ruling at $68 per barrel and rising. From 2011 to 2013, it ruled at more than $100 per barrel. This was leading to a rise in the prices of petrol and diesel in the international market. Our domestic prices were also rising accordingly; it was putting pressure on the demand for domestic coal, as coal prices were in sync with oil's in the global marketplace.

India Spring: Movement against Corruption

Meanwhile, a separate narrative was being built on corruption in the government. All countries with low per capita incomes, including India, suffer from this problem. Institutional reforms and technology are used by them to minimize the malady. But the millions of poor who are the victims of this cancer of corruption are extremely conscious of this disease and have a strong dislike for corrupt politicians, bureaucrats and government machinery.

The UPA was now gradually being attacked in this area. After the allotment of 122 telecom licences in January 2008, there were allegations of wrongdoing against the government. A case was registered by the CBI in October 2009 against unknown officers of the Department of Telecommunications (DoT) and unknown private persons/companies under various provisions of the Indian Penal Code and Prevention of Corruption Act. The office of the DoT was raided by the CBI. It was clear that while A. Raja, the then telecom minister, was not named in the FIR, he would have to answer the charges sooner or later, which led to strained relations with the DMK. Raja finally resigned after more than a year. In November 2009, the CBI sought details of the taped conversations of Niira Radia, a corporate lobbyist, to determine the involvement of middlemen in the grant of these licences.

In November 2010, the CAG gave a report about this allotment and mentioned a presumptive loss of up to ₹1.76 lakh crore to the government. The figures of loss were highly inflated and the concept of presumptive loss was foreign to the mandate of the CAG. (We will analyse this issue in the next chapter.)

When the Constitution of the country was adopted more than seven decades back, the founding fathers had hoped its various organs would function in accordance with the highest traditions of democracy. Speaking about this, Dr Ambedkar, in his speech delivered in the constituent Assembly in November 1949, had said:

> The working of the Constitution does not depend wholly upon
> the nature of the Constitution. The Constitution can provide

only the organs of State such as the Legislature, the Executive and the Judiciary. The factors on which the working of these organs of State depends are the people and the political parties they will set up as their instruments to carry out their wishes and their politics.*

A well-functioning democracy requires all its institutions to work in accordance with its recognized principles, norms and traditions. The boundaries of their power are clearly laid down in the Constitution and have evolved over the past seven decades. In the past two decades, however, there have been occasions when the institutions have gone beyond these boundaries. This was another such occasion. The report from a well-respected institution like the CAG provided a very strong base for the belief that the government was engaged in corrupt behaviour. Normally, this would have gone unnoticed, as audit is not an area in which the common man is normally interested. This, however, impacted a vital sector of the economy which was critical for economic growth.

Over the next three years, from 2010 to 2012, there were intensive discussions in the media about corruption in the government. This was fuelled by several incidents. The Commonwealth Games (CWG) were being organized in Delhi and several stadiums and the Games Village had to be completed in time, by October 2010. There was a serious time overrun. There were reports of irregularities, wastage of money and corruption.** Suresh Kalmadi, chairman

---

*http://shodhganga.inflibnet.ac.in/bitstream/10603/38799/15/15_appendix.pdf
**PTI, 'Major scam hits Commonwealth Games', *The Hindu*, 31 July 2010, accessed 23 March 2019, https://www.thehindu.com/news/national/Major-scam-hits-Commonwealth-Games/article16215706.ece

of the CWG organizing committee, was arrested in April 2011. Other developments, such as the Radia tapes and the Adarsh Housing Society scam, only reinforced the belief that there was huge corruption in the governance system. In March 2012, the CAG, Vinod Rai, presented yet another report in which there was no circumvention by use of the phrase 'presumptive loss'. He computed a loss to the government of ₹1.86 lakh crore due to the allocation of coal blocks to private investors. These allocations had been made during 2005–09 to enable them to get fuel for power plants, cement plants and iron and steel production. This report further intensified criticism against the government. It was now believed that faulty policies of the Central government had caused a loss to the exchequer of more than ₹3.5 lakh crore. This was huge, and reinforced the impression that there was large-scale corruption in the government. The methodology for calculating these losses in the CAG report was beyond its remit and unsustainable. And yet it had a key role in fuelling the perception of corruption in the government. In fact, later, when the matter went to court, no criminality was found in the 2G case filed earlier by the CBI.

Meanwhile, a movement to set up a Lokpal had begun. In 2011 it gathered a lot of momentum. India Against Corruption (IAC), an organization set up by a group of individuals—including Santosh Hegde, a former judge of the SC—started a non-political movement for setting up a Lokpal in the country in accordance with a draft of the Jan Lokpal Bill prepared by them. The Lokpal was expected to be in the nature of the Ombudsman, helping control corruption, especially in high places. It got the support of Anna Hazare, a Gandhian from Maharashtra who had excellent credentials. To maintain pressure, Hazare started his fast at Jantar Mantar in Delhi in April that year. After five days and some informal talks, the fast was called off. The government agreed to set up a joint committee of government ministers and the civil society to draft a Bill to set up a Lokpal. Pranab Mukherjee, the minister of finance then, was to preside over the committee with the former law minister Shanti Bhushan as co-chair. This was an unusual arrangement to develop legislation and clearly indicated that the government was under immense pressure. It was reflective of the unusual times.

There were now efforts on to show that the government was not serious about eradicating corruption. In May 2011, India had ratified the UN Convention against Corruption. This contained provisions for cooperation among countries to provide assistance in seizing financial assets associated with corrupt earnings. Baba Ramdev, under the banner of Bharat Swabhiman Trust, started a movement demanding that all the money Indians had deposited in Swiss Banks—the amount mentioned by him was huge—be brought back. He decided to hold a meeting in Delhi at the vast Ramlila Maidan to intensify his movement. Government ministers met him, but he was not dissuaded. His protest was to last for forty days. But the government cancelled permission for this meeting and arrested his followers in a raid; Ramdev fled to Haridwar. During this period, hundreds of youth and other well-meaning individuals visited the Ramlila Maidan.

By July, talks between the civil society group of Hazare and the government had broken down. Two versions of the Lokpal Bill had emerged. Hazare, meanwhile, announced a fast from 16 August to exert more pressure on the government to accept their version of the Bill. He, along with his followers, was arrested as a preventive measure, but, with mounting nationwide criticism, had to be quickly released. However, Hazare refused to leave Tihar Jail unless he was allowed to fast and his demands accepted. He finally left three days later, after the government agreed to let him undertake his fast at the Ramlila Maidan. While I had no idea of any ongoing political interventions to resolve the issue, my colleague Saumitra Chaudhuri, a member of the Planning Commission, mentioned to me the possibility of Vilasrao Deshmukh's intervention. Saumitra had good contacts in many circles in Mumbai. Later, Deshmukh, a Union minister and also the former CM of Maharashtra, had a long interaction with Hazare. Deshmukh's was a critical intervention in resolving the issue and reaching a settlement with the Gandhian.

There was massive support for Hazare, with nearly one lakh people turning up on a Sunday at the Ramlila Maidan. In the ongoing negotiations, Hazare raised three demands: a citizens' charter, covering the entire bureaucracy under the Lokpal Bill, and the setting up of similar institutions in the states. The issue was debated in the Parliament and a resolution was passed in the Lok Sabha unanimously accepting these demands. Hazare continued his fast for twelve days and fixed a fresh deadline in December 2011 for the enactment of the Bill.

The parliamentary standing committee, meanwhile, gave its report. Hazare held a demonstration in early December against this, as the report was not in full conformity with his demands. Later, the government introduced the Lokpal Bill in the Rajya Sabha on the last day of the session in December. The Bill was finally passed by the Parliament in December 2013.

Despite strong public support for the setting up of the institution of Lokpal, its actual appointment has taken six long years. Clearly, the NDA government was not very enthusiastic about it. Ultimately, it was the SC that had to force its hand. Pinaki Chandra Ghose, a former judge of the SC, became the first Lokpal on 19 March 2019. Eight other members were also appointed. This is a major development in our fight against corruption in high places, particularly among the Central ministers and senior civil servants. Hopefully, it will also put an end to the misuse of anticorruption agencies like the CBI and the ED by the government in power.

Interestingly, the IAC movement has now completely disappeared, possibly due to a lack of funds, and corruption continues as before. Some of the key supporters of the IAC have now joined politics. The media, which earlier seemed to roar at the ills of corruption, is not discussing the issue with any vigour any more. Meanwhile, India, for the past three years, has been sliding down the ranking of Transparency International, a global organization leading the fight against corruption, and is worse off than China in 2017.

Coal: A Full Stop to Growth

While the corruption narrative was impacting governance, the demand for coal was rapidly increasing. In view of the high international prices of energy, which rose sharply in 2009–2014, the power, steel and cement industry demanded domestic coal, which was moderately priced. The domestic availability, however, could not increase partly due to the government policy on environment and later due to problems in coal mining arising from the CAG report and PILs related to coal. This had serious consequences for power plants and the banks that had lent money to power companies.

Let me first describe how the demand for coal went up so sharply in just five years (2004–2009). It was driven primarily by the power sector. In 2007, when I joined the Planning Commission and looked at the power sector, I was concerned about the huge gap between the supply of power and its demand. There was a massive shortage of power. In the earlier plans, we had set targets for power generation but there were huge shortfalls, as various policy instruments were not in place. In particular, the private sector had taken time to prepare and was not ready. Most of the generation was coal-based in those days. Growth of hydel power was slow and there were serious problems with environment clearance, land acquisition and strong opposition from some NGOs. Solar and wind power were in their infancy. Technology on solar-power generation was still evolving and the cost of such power in 2007 was as high as ₹15–₹17 per unit, as against power from other sources such as coal, at ₹2.5–₹3.5 per unit. To reduce the demand-supply gap, we had kept a rather ambitious target of about 88,000 MW of new power plants for the Eleventh Plan. The major constraint was availability of coal, based on which most of the capacities were coming up.

The demand for coal from Coal India Limited (CIL) increased rapidly as economic growth accelerated. While only 55,000 MW power capacity could be set up for generation during the Eleventh Plan (2007–2012), in the next plan we had planned for a capacity of 88,000 MW. More and more coal-based power plants supported by state governments started coming up. The coal companies were expected to increase the average growth rate of production to 9.4 per cent, up from 6 per cent in the Tenth Plan, which had finished in

2006–07. The Eleventh Plan expected a major growth in production from captive mines too to meet the demand-supply gap. It projected a production of nearly 100 million tonnes from private coal mines, both new and existing. This was nearly six times of what had been achieved at the end of the Tenth Plan, but even this was not expected to meet the full demand of the sharply rising growth. We expected to import nearly 50 million tonnes to meet this demand. The plan reflected a clear assessment that it was not possible to meet the entire demand of the economy from government mines alone and that strong support of production from captive mines was needed.

The issue of coal shortage from domestic production was often discussed in the infrastructure meetings or in the Cabinet when these problems came up for discussion. The coal secretary would be often asked to expedite the allocation of blocks for captive mining, so that the availability of coal from domestic mines could be augmented. In 1993, the government had decided to permit the allocation of coal blocks to captive power plants and steel units by amending the Coal Mines (Nationalization) Act (CMNA), 1973. Later, this was extended to cement units too. The allocation of such blocks was to be decided on the recommendation of a committee in the Ministry of Coal, which had representatives from other user ministries, the railways, the state governments and the technical experts deciding on applications received. This was called the screening committee and was headed by the additional secretary or the secretary in the Ministry of Coal. The mining leases were to be issued by the state government in all such cases, as required under the Mines and Minerals (Development and Regulation) Act, 1957. The government, realizing that this approach may not meet the demands of the economy, formed a committee under Professor K.R. Chari, a coal expert, to suggest further measures. This committee recommended that the best option was the commercial mining of coal, so that it could be available to all sectors. A Bill to amend the CMNA was introduced in the Parliament accordingly in 2000 by the Vajpayee-led NDA government amid strong opposition by the trade Unions and Left parties. In view of this strong opposition, the government did not press the issue and the Bill remained pending in Parliament, a defunct document for all practical purposes. As a result of this, the system of captive mining allocation on the recommendations of the screening committee continued.

Efforts to step up production by CIL met with serious problems after the first two years of the Eleventh Plan. The growth of production by CIL dropped sharply. The new minister in 2009 for Environment, Forest and Climate Change suddenly put in place policies that practically stopped growth in coal production. The coal-bearing areas were classified into two categories—'Go' and 'No Go'. The implication of this policy was that no environment clearances would be given to the 'No Go' areas. All mining henceforth was to be confined to the 'Go' areas. In these areas where mining was allowed, restrictions were put on expanding mine capacities in practically all major mine complexes of CIL on the grounds that the air quality was already bad. This had a disastrous effect on coal production. For two years, until March 2011, production by CIL remained stagnant at about 431 million tonnes, as against the earlier growth of about 7 per cent per annum in the first two years of the plan. Even in the captive mines, there was very little growth. Production in the terminal year of the plan, in 2011–12, increased to 36 million tonnes, as against 17.5 million tonnes in the terminal year 2006–07 of the previous plan. I discussed the issue with the minister of environment, forest and climate change, but he was unrelenting. This had serious consequences for the economy.

A number of power plants and steel units that had already made investments were now stuck. While coal production was practically stagnant in CIL mines, any possibility of increase from private mines disappeared after the CAG report. As mentioned earlier, it reported a massive financial loss to the government in the allocation of coal blocks to private captive power, steel or cement plants. In the media there was severe criticism of these allocations. Separately, the CVC asked the CBI to inquire into the complaints of coal block allocation. Based on all this, two PILs were filed in the SC alleging corruption and requesting cancellation of the blocks. During the hearing, after a request was made by one of the parties, the court directed that the CBI investigation in the coal-block-allocation cases be court-monitored. I recall an occasion when there was a report that the law minister had called the CBI director and discussed with him the progress of the case. Promptly, it was alleged that the minister was trying to influence the investigation, causing a lot of embarrassment to the government. In an atmosphere where the officials of the Ministry of Coal were under CBI investigation, the allocation of coal blocks to private players was being treated as a massive loss to the public exchequer, the SC was considering the cancellation of captive block allocation and no private player was willing to invest money in developing these blocks. In such an atmosphere, the production of coal grew nominally. The annual growth in coal production between 2010–11 and 2013–14 went down sharply and averaged just 1.1 per cent, as against 6.7 per cent between 2004–05 and 2009–2010. This was disastrous for the economy, as there were new plants coming up but no coal from domestic sources.

In view of the shortage of coal, the government worked out a formula that amounted to rationing of coal. Taking note of the shortage in supply by CIL and Singareni Collieries Company Limited (SCCL), another government coal-mining company, to meet the full commitment of the contracted quantity to power plants, the government decided to fix a minimum level for the Annual Contracted Quantity (ACQ), supply of which was to be ensured by the coal companies. It was only much later that a more satisfactory position emerged, primarily due to higher production in the CIL and SCCL mines.

A Battle of Perception

The perception of huge corruption in the government had negative consequences for both governance and democracy. The credibility of the government was seriously damaged. The Opposition parties led by the BJP disrupted several sessions of the Parliament. This created an impression that our system was non-functional. The CBI investigations and monitoring by the SC implied that the government was interfering in a fair investigation or was likely to. This further lowered the image of the government in the public eye. After the start of criminal investigation against secretaries to the Government of India in coal, 2G and other cases, civil servants were worried about their own protection while taking tough decisions. Many decisions even got delayed, leading to a perceived 'policy paralysis'.

Global experience has been that in all countries with low per capita incomes, like India, there is a medium to high degree of corruption prevalent in society. Such countries work on new institutions and norms to curb the misuse of public money, bring transparency and minimize corruption. India was engaged in a similar process. The CAG's reports, however, hinted at levels of corruption that were far from reality, and it seemed that it was aimed at drawing public attention to itself. It has caused enormous harm to the integrity of our governance system and has had serious consequences for the quality of public discourse.

The UPA-II had come to power with a bigger majority than the UPA-I. With its commitment to stick to the nuclear deal, it was considered a strong government. It, however, lost the corruption narrative. The issue of telecom licences and coal-block allocation highlighted by the CAG were taken up by the media, judges and political parties. Surprisingly, there was no analysis of some of the absurdities of the CAG reports, nor did any institution care that the CAG's loss-to-exchequer figure was based on his own framing of the government policy on the issue. In the long run, these developments in our society and polity adversely impacted the national economy.

Chapter 8

THE CAG'S OVERREACH

In one of my meetings with the PM in the last week of November 2010, he remarked that the government was facing a lot of criticism on the issue of telecom licences. I pointed out that the telecom policy was the prerogative of the government and not of auditors. But if there had been a mistake in its implementation, it needed to be corrected. He asked me to see him the next day.

I was able to obtain a copy of the CAG report from a colleague and gather more facts. I also rang up the late Dr J.S. Sarma, who was then the chairman of the Telecom Regulatory Authority of India (TRAI), and had a long discussion with him to fully appreciate the nuances of the issue. The report had highlighted two major issues. The first was that the 122 telecom licences issued in January 2008 to various private players were in contravention of the government's avowed policy of issuing such licences on a first-come-first-served (FCFS) basis or issuing them in the order in which they had applied for the licence; thus, those who had applied earlier should have got priority. The second was that the government had incurred a loss (the CAG referred to it as 'presumptive loss') that had been estimated by the CAG to be in the range of ₹33,000 crore and ₹1.76 lakh crore, as it had not increased the fee for new telecom licensees given in 2008 to reflect the changed market conditions in the seven years after 2001 when the fee had been fixed. The government charged a fee for entry and spectrum. With the increased number of mobile users in the country, spectrum was in short supply for new connections. The CAG said that the government should have charged higher prices for spectrum to reflect this shortage. The report had drawn strong public attention and criticism of the government due to the high loss of revenue to the government it showed.

I explained to the PM the contraventions of the FCFS policy mentioned by the CAG and their implications. The CAG had pointed out three major contraventions of this policy:

- ✕ The number of licences were sought to be artificially restricted by announcing that only those who had applied by 1 October 2007 would be given a licence; later this was changed to 25 September 2007 for no clear reason. This was against the TRAI recommendation too.
- ✕ The FCFS policy was tweaked. Generally, after a decision had been made to issue telecom licences, the government would issue letters of intent (LoIs). In it, private players would be asked to complete certain formalities so that they could get their licences. This included giving a performance bank guarantee (PBG) and a financial bank guarantee (FBG). They were generally given fifteen days to do so. But the priority in the actual issuing of the licence was

always FCFS. The government changed this policy priority to those who completed the formalities of the LoI first. This was beneficial to those who, by some unethical means, had envisaged these changes. Also, old applicants lost priority.

✗ Eighty-five licences were given to companies that were ineligible, as they did not satisfy the basic criterion set by the DoT, and suppressed facts, disclosed incomplete information and submitted fake documents for getting the licence and spectrum.

I suggested that if licences had been issued in contravention of the existing government policy, these needed to be cancelled. The PM was worried not about others but primarily about where foreign investors had put in their money. What about India's image as a country with attractive opportunities and stable FDI policies? I recalled, however, the case of a large number of petrol-dealer licences issued in 2003. These were done by committees that, in many cases, were chaired by judges and had senior retired officials. Once it was realized that irregularities had occurred in this, all the licences had been cancelled. The issue had finally gone to the SC and only 40 per cent of the licences were found to be in order; the rest stood cancelled. But this demonstrated the government's willingness to act in accordance with the norms. I told the PM we needed a similar approach.

The PM asked me to give him a note on the options we had open to us. In the note, prepared in consultation with the chairman of TRAI, I suggested the cancellation of the eighty-five licences that had been found to be in violation of the norms and given to ineligible companies. I suggested that further action be taken after receiving the report of the Public Accounts Committee (PAC) on the issue. Gracious as ever, next time I met him, he thanked me for a 'very useful note'.

The approach I had suggested had another advantage. My past experience was that in all such cases, the licensee would approach the SC and allege gross injustice. The court would listen to it and the government would be criticized for being too harsh on new players—and the entire debate in the public space would be diverted from the present anti-government stance.

I have no idea what happened to my note. Possibly, it went to the DoT, following which the government decided to set up the One-Man Committee (OMC) under Justice (Retired) Shivraj Patil, a former judge of the SC, to examine the appropriateness of the procedures followed by the DoT in the issue of licences and the allocation of spectrum during 2001–09 and give its recommendation. Thus the department went on to examine the lacunae in the licence-allotment issues of earlier regimes as well. Justice Patil gave his report in about forty-five days. He found serious deficiencies in the FCFS policy, in the additional spectrum allocation and the non-revision of charges when the market was changing.

The government failed to realize that by handling the issue in this manner, it would only be tarnishing the image of the earlier Vajpayee-led NDA government. It would, however, not solve the problems arising from the wrongdoings referred to by the CAG in the present case. The only way to handle it was to correct the mistakes made suo moto. The 122 licences given in contravention of policy and, in some cases, obtained through use of questionable means—or at least the eighty-five licences given to ineligible companies—should have been cancelled by the government and not as part of as SC order.

The SC by its order dated 2 February 2012 cancelled the above licences. In its order it observed:

> The manner in which the exercise for grant of LoIs to the applicants was conducted on 10.1.2008 leaves no room for doubt that everything was stage-managed to favour those who were able to know in advance the change in the implementation of the first-come-first-served policy. As a result of this, some of the companies which had submitted applications in 2004 or 2006 were pushed down in the priority and those who had applied between August and September 2007 succeeded in getting higher seniority, entitling them to allocation of spectrum on priority basis.*

A Disastrous Approach

The CAG report in the 2G case raised questions that had serious implications for governance and its approach to audit. While the CAG was correct in pointing out the errors in the allocation of licences, he also raised the issue of presumptive loss, which was taken as loss to government revenue. All losses are computed based on government policy when a decision is taken. It is the prerogative of all governments to price their resources. This is part of public

---

*'Full text: Supreme Court order on 2G scam', News18.com, 2 February 2012, accessed 8 April 2019, https://www.news18.com/news/india/full-text-supreme-court-order-on-2g-scam-442963.html

policy. Many pricing structures are, at times, below the market price. This may be necessary to stimulate economic growth or expand the reach of services. Services like primary education are free and health services are highly subsidized. In public distribution, foodgrains are free to a large section of the public. Drinking water, a natural resource, is highly subsidized. In a welfare state, this prerogative of the government cannot be questioned.

The objective of the New Telecom Policy (NTP) 1999 was to provide access to telecommunications for the achievement of the country's social and economic goals. The availability of affordable and effective communication for citizens was considered at the core of the vision and goal of the policy. It strived to provide a balance between the provision of universal service to all uncovered areas, including the rural areas, and the provision of high-level services capable of meeting the needs of the country's economy. In pursuance of this objective, private investment was invited and a lot of investment was done in developing and expanding the infrastructure sector.

The government policy since 2001 was to get for itself an entry fee and prescribed share of revenues to be earned by the new telecom licence, and to provide licence along with spectrum to private players to run the business. Spectrum was priced moderately. This led to massive expansion of telecom, from a mere 5.5 crore connections in 2003 to 62 crore connections in 2010. This increased further to nearly 100 crore by March 2015.*

---

*Telecom Statistics, India-2017, Economic Research Unit, Department of Telecommunications, Ministry of Communications, Government of India, New Delhi, accessed 26 March 2019
http://dot.gov.in/sites/default/files/Telecom%20Statistics%20India-2017.

This surge in growth had not happened in any other sector and had wider implications for the economy, which benefited extensively in terms of jobs, affordable communication for millions of poor, and a new governance mechanism to reach villages and deliver public services. The faster growth resulted in a positive impact on the GDP, which had long-term benefits in terms of extra revenue for the government. The government clearly exercised a wise choice by going for revenue-share and by pricing spectrum moderately, thus expanding the market rather than fixing prices at very high rates and killing the golden telecom goose.

The government decided against raising the spectrum charges for new licensees. The CAG felt that this was wrong and hence computed loss to the government based on the market value of spectrum. By computing presumptive loss as loss to the government, the CAG tried to usurp the government's role in making public policy. While doing so, he did not take a broad and more comprehensive economic view of the issue in assessing the policies of the telecom sector.

By deviating from the time-honoured principle of computing losses to the government based on difference between the pricing fixed by the government and the price actually charged, the CAG, by arriving at a sale price he thought should have been fixed, brought in uncertainty to the auditing process, as the exercise involved discovering the market value of the telecom licences given in violation of the FCFS policy. Even in normal times, discovering the market price of any product is a difficult exercise. It is not like commodities, where there are well-known hubs such as S&P Global

pdf?download=1

Platts, commonly called Platt, for crude oil. For products, it is far more difficult. As a result, his calculation of the market value of loss showed a wide variation, ranging from about ₹33,000 crore to ₹1.76 lakh crore. It almost appeared as if the CAG wanted to exaggerate the figure of loss, treating the public as his audience rather than the PAC when he used the figure of 3G auctions held in 2010 to compute losses in licence given in early 2008. Market access was changing fast and growing at the rate of about 40 per cent per annum in 2003–2010. The type of 2G services was quite different from 3G, which included data. So neither were the market conditions of 2010 comparable to that of early 2008, nor was the type of spectrum allotted, viz. 3G, comparable to the allocations made to new licences. And yet this was chosen as an estimate of loss.

By moving into the realm of market value of telecom licences rather than sticking to the audited numbers of accounts, the CAG entered an area that needed a more comprehensive assessment than had been done before. If market value were to be assigned to the new licensees, the growth of the telecom market could take a different trajectory. Wherever possible, the new players would try to recover the cost by focusing on value-added services instead of mere expansion. This could slow down growth and the access of common citizens to these services. The overall growth of the economy and governance benefits could be impacted. Thus a comparison of loss required a more comprehensive assessment, including economic impact in the two scenarios: one with the rates on which allocation was made and the other based on different market values identified and indicated by the CAG. The cost-benefit comparison would then yield the implication of the decision to award the licences at the rates prevalent so far. Even this analysis would involve a lot of assumptions. With different assumptions, the results would be different. The CAG thus entered an area that had large uncertainties.

There was also the question of equity, which was ignored by both the CAG and the SC in its judgement. All the earlier licensees had paid an entry fee and were annually paying a revenue share towards the licence fee and spectrum usage. While getting the licence, a start-up spectrum had been bundled along with it. The new licensees had to have similar terms so as to be able to provide competition, which was in the interest of consumers. But the CAG ignored this issue in his report. How the competition was going to be on a level playing field and thus fair was not considered at all.

It is interesting to note that the trial court of CBI in its judgement of 21 December 2017 found all the allegations baseless and held the following view:

> There is no evidence on the record produced before the court indicating any criminality in the acts allegedly committed by the accused persons relating to fixation of cut-off date, manipulation of first-come-first-served policy, allocation of spectrum to dual technology applicants, ignoring ineligibility of STPL and Unitech group companies, non-revision of entry fee and transfer of Rs. 200 crore to Kalaignar TV (P) Limited as illegal gratification.*

---

*ANI, '2G spectrum case judgement: Here's what court said in its verdict', *Deccan Chronicle*, 21 December 2017, accessed 8 April 2019, https://www.deccanchronicle.com/nation/current-affairs/211217/2g-spectrum-case-judgement-heres-what-court-said-in-its-verdict.html

The CAG's Blunders in the Coal Saga

In May 2012, the CAG gave a report in which he criticized the government's allocation of coal blocks to private and government companies. In its report, the CAG used the cost of production of CIL mines and their sale price as the basis for computing the profits and argued that the private-sector captive-mine allottees had got this gain. He computed a huge benefit of ₹1.86 lakh crore to private parties who were allotted these blocks.* He argued that by delaying the operationalizing of competitive bidding since 2004—when a decision was taken in a meeting attended by the coal secretary to undertake competitive bidding—the private mine owners had benefited to the above extent and some of this revenue could have accrued to the government. The CAG also traced the history of the proposal for competitive bidding of auctioning the blocks for captive use in the government and argued that this method was more transparent and should be used. He did not evaluate all allocations, but as a sample identified the allocation of the Fatehpur and the Rampia captive coal blocks and found the procedure of selection by a committee non-transparent. The report was hailed by many as a massive unearthing of corruption in the government system and was referred to as Coalgate.

However, there are serious concerns about the issues raised in

---

*Audit has estimated financial gains to the tune of ₹1.86 lakh crore likely to accrue to private coal-block allottees (based on average cost of production and average sale price of open cast mines of CIL in 2010–2011). And also that a part of this financial gain could have accrued to the national exchequer by operationalizing the decision taken years earlier to introduce competitive bidding for the allocation of coal blocks.

the report. The CAG tried to enter the domain of policymaking, which is not the remit of the CAG but of the government. Many of its findings were derived from first assuming what the government policy should have been and then computing profits to the private sector. The CAG failed to realize that when captive coal allocation was permitted by the legislature in 1993, there was no computation of how much profit the captive-mine allotees could derive, beyond which they would have to surrender any extra gain to the government. The objective of the legislation was to expand economic activity by providing a window for coal availability to private power plants, and cement and steel plants which were being set up. The government was not looking to prescribing a separate balance sheet for captive coal-mining blocks. It was to be just a power plant that had the captive coal block for its use. To argue that the government should have used it for getting some revenues directly was clearly not in accordance with the original intention of the legislation. Of course, the increased economic activity with this policy approach would have given higher revenues to the government in due course.

The report also did not fully appreciate the overall economic logic of the decision made by the government in 1993, but focused on direct revenues from the coal block auction rather than on the huge overall economic benefits and revenues that would flow from it. In the 1990s, India was just coming out of a massive financial crisis. The government had, therefore, opened up the economy and invited private investment. It had decided in 1992 to invite the private sector to set up new power capacities. As an incentive and to support this initiative, it decided in 1993 to amend the CMNA 1973 to permit captive coal mines to be allocated to private investors.

The objective of the Bill was to provide coal for power generation and other industries. While allocating captive mines or permitting private power plants, it was expected that the private sector would mine the coal efficiently, save costs, improve efficiency and invest in the economy. In fact, efficiency was the watchword for economic growth as India liberalized its economy for the private sector in a large number of areas. The government was looking at the larger picture and not just focusing on this exercise as a revenue-raising item from coal-block auction. The approach was that the private sector would make profits and invest in the economy.

This was nothing new. For long periods, governments had been providing natural resources like land and water, and even tax concessions, to attract industries in most states. Prior to this, governments had allocated iron ore mines and coal blocks for its use to develop the steel industry. In the mining sector, the government had raised resources from royalties from coal and other minerals. The broad approach was to allocate natural resources and get the best economic advantage out of it. There was no restriction on the efficient running of coal mines by a private investor so as to maximize profits from the steel, cement and power sectors and develop a competitive industrial base.

The CAG report ignored the way decision-making is done in governments and came from a position which was, strictly speaking, factually incorrect. All governments discuss various proposals and ideas over a period. A policy emerges quite often after a very long time. It is the nature of democracy and of our federal system.

There was no decision in 2004 to introduce competitive bidding. The view expressed by the coal secretary in a meeting at the PMO that coal blocks be given on a competitive bidding basis was only his personal view. The decision required changes in the Act, and approval by the Cabinet. It required consultation with the states. To term a decision taken at a meeting as a 'government decision' is clearly incorrect. And to argue for operationalizing it when there was no such decision is difficult to understand. The argument that the intention was clear in 2004, and that the government lost revenue because of delay in giving it formal shape is completely untenable. To start computing losses or profits based on the time taken for a certain decision because of internal government processes is a flawed approach.

If this policy is adopted across the board, there could be disastrous consequences. Imagine the discussions that have gone on for more than a decade in the implementation of the Goods and Services Tax (GST). Experts believe that the loss to the economy is 1–2 per cent of lower GDP. I recall a study done by us for the Thirteenth Finance Commission when similar numbers were given. Over a five-year period, the loss to national wealth could be nearly $100–200 billion. But we don't start filing charge sheets because of this. It has to be understood that in a democracy and federal system, decision-making is often tortuous. And this cannot be the basis for computing losses or profits. If consultations took time and the nature of polity was such that the government finally decided to use the auction method only later, it was certainly not good governance. But the auditors exceeded their mandate when they calculated losses in revenue to the government based on a policy that they thought should have been adopted by the government rather than the policy that was in place since 1993.

The CAG's core argument was a bit far-fetched on another count. It made an assumption that the coal from the entire mine had been extracted by the mine owners and that the coal was available for sale and would fetch a price that was being realized by CIL. While normally in such cases where revenues occur over a period of years, the concept of 'net present value', or NPV, is used, the CAG did not consider it necessary to do so. As a result, the gains were indicative of a highly inflated figure. If this concept, which is accepted when revenue streams flow over a period, were to be used, the so-called benefits would go down to less than half of the computation made by the CAG. After making other adjustments on the quality of coal and the e-auction, it would further go down to about one-fourth.*

The CAG has also erred in observing that the allocation of captive coal blocks was not transparent. The crux of the matter was whether in the given system, it was fair. The method used for this purpose, as in many other areas, was of an interministerial committee with representation from all the concerned states. Such a method of selection is used widely in many areas, and the intention in these meetings is to consider the views of all stakeholders and then decide the best option for the sector. This method is used for selecting almost all senior-level appointments, secretaries to the government, chairmen of public-sector undertakings, members of regulatory commissions

---

*There were other shortcomings in computation too. The type of coal available in most of these allotted captive mines was expected to be of inferior quality, given the area where these mines were situated. This would have fetched a much lower price if mined. Also, it was estimated that the surplus was inflated due to the e-auction coal income/production not being discounted, which provided nearly 20–25 per cent of the income from 10 per cent of production only. Discounting these factors for working averages, the estimate of gain to private players would only be 20 per cent of the figure estimated by the CAG. It is not clear why these basic factors were ignored when arriving at the 'loss' figure.

and, in fact, the bulk of senior selections. Universities use it extensively for selecting professors and other high teaching positions. In all such cases, only decisions are recorded without an analysis of factors leading to a selection. In this case, there were a large number of applicants and the two main stakeholders of the government, namely the state where the unit was to be set up and the ministry responsible for the growth of the sector, were represented.

So when the committee took a view considering the overall picture, it was acting in the best interests of the sector. There were practically no representations against these decisions. There were so many factors—including availability of land and water, past record and financial health of the company, and the availability or the possibility of technical personnel being available—that a good evaluation was possible after interministerial discussions by making a broad overall assessment. Thereafter, it was hardly possible to prepare a comparative analysis of why someone did or did not get a coal block. This was a reasonable method, though, like all other decisions, an element of subjectivity was inevitable. However, to argue that a well-reasoned speaking order should have been part of the proceedings is to misconstrue the role of the committee. It was not a judicial or even a quasi-judicial body, but an administrative committee of the government. I am not aware of such committees passing a quasi-judicial order.

Coalgate in Court

After the scathing CAG report, the SC on 25 August 2014 passed an order cancelling 214 of the 218 coal-block allocations. Later, in a judgement as a follow-up of the findings, it awarded a penalty of ₹295 per tonne on the coal mined by the private companies from the blocks allocated to them. It held that there was no provision in the law for allocation of coal blocks by the Central government. It also held that the allocation under Section 3(3) of the CMNA 1973 as amended was contemplated for units engaged in power generation or production of iron and steel or cement, and not meant to cover those units which were only planning to do so. It further found serious lacunae in the selection of firms to which the blocks had been allotted on the grounds of it being non-transparent, not permissible (to allot a block to a group of firms with one of them as a group leader) and not in accordance with any fixed norms. It also interpreted the provisions of Section 3(3)(a)(i) of the CMNA 1973 in a manner that only Central government companies or corporations were entitled to mining under the provision. It thus held that a state government or its PSUs or joint-venture companies were not entitled to coal mining under that provision.

The court's view that the Central government did not have powers to allot coal blocks came in 2014. It has to be realized that prior to that, for nearly two decades, the process as understood was that the Central government allocated the blocks and the mining licence was issued by the state government. There was no objection by state governments to this process and no representation made from other stakeholders. Why not lay the law for the future, particularly since the government itself had amended the Act in 2010 and introduced competitive bidding? Why cancel nearly 50 per cent of the blocks given to state governments or state PSUs? Apart from the overall approach of the court in cancelling the blocks and its severe adverse consequences for the power and steel sectors, there are also serious concerns about several interpretations of the provisions of the CMNA 1973 by the court. Several of its findings on the interpretation of the CMNA need a review.*

The court had also not fully considered the implications of the different provisions of the CMNA 1973 before arriving at the finding that the state companies and corporations were not entitled to coal mining under Section 3(3)(a)(i) of the Act. In particular, it had not considered the definition of the terms used in Section 3(3) of the CMNA. The provisions read as follows:

Section 3(3)

a. no person other than

   i. the Central Government or a Government Company or a corporation owned, managed or controlled by the Central Government, or

   ii ....

   iii ....

   Shall carry out mining operation in India.**

Thus a 'government company' can clearly carry out mining. The definition of a government company has been given as follows under Section 2 of the above Act, where all terms used in the CMNA have been defined:

---

*A detailed analysis is available on several of these issues related to the period 2003–05 and before in an excellent book *The Coal Conundrum: Executive Failure and Judicial Arrogance* by P.C. Parakh, former coal secretary in the Government of India.

**https://coal.nic.in/sites/upload_files/coal/files/curentnotices/act1973_0_0.pdf

Section 2(f): A Government Company has the meaning assigned to it by the Section 617 of the Companies Act 1956.*

Under Section 617 of the Companies Act, the government companies are defined as:

[Those] in which not less than fifty one per cent of the paid up share capital is held by the Central Government, or by any State Government or Governments.**

Thus, all PSUs of the Central and state governments are covered by the definition of a 'government company'. The court did not consider this complete meaning, which was given in the definition section of the Act. Clearly, the findings of the court need review on this count.

Another argument contained in the above judgement to support the cancellation of the coal blocks was about the nature of the companies that were entitled to get captive mines. The court took a very restrictive interpretation of the provisions regarding companies that could do coal mining. The provision of Section 3(3)(a)(iii) reads:

Section 3(3)(a): no person, other than –

(i) ....

(ii) ....

(iii) a company engaged in –

    (1) the production of iron and steel

    (2) generation of power

    (3) washing of coal obtained from a mine, or

---

*https://coal.nic.in/sites/upload_files/coal/files/curentnotices/act1973_0_0.pdf
**http://www.mca.gov.in/Ministry/pdf/Companies_Act_1956_13jun2011.pdf

(4) such other end use as the Central Government may, by notification, specify shall carry on coal mining operation in India in any form*

The court took a view that the word 'engaged in' implied that the company applying for the coal block must have set up an iron or steel plant, power or cement plant and be engaged in the production of steel, power or cement. The prospective engagement by a private company in the production of steel, power or cement would not entitle such a private company to carry out coal-mining operations.

The above view is unsustainable on several grounds. Prior to Independence, there were several private companies, notably in Calcutta (now Kolkata), Ahmedabad and Bombay (now Mumbai), engaged in the generation of power. After the Electricity (Supply) Act, 1948, several private companies were taken in the public sector, and later, SEBs were set up to put new generation capacities and manage the power sector. The amendment to the Electricity (Supply) Act, 1948, was made only in 1991 to permit private players to set up power plants in the private sector. Thus, in this sector, the policy for private investments was finalized only in 1992. So when the amendments to the CMNA were done in 1993, it was specifically mentioned that the intention was to provide captive coal blocks for the proposed power stations. The following extract from the statement of object and reason of the 1993 amendment to the CMNA clearly mentions this:

---

*https://coal.nic.in/sites/upload_files/coal/files/curentnotices/act1973_0_0.pdf

As an alternative, it is proposed to offer new coal and lignite mines to the proposed power stations in the private sector for the purpose of captive end use.*

The 1993 amendment was a follow-up of the opening of the power sector for private investment and 100 per cent FDI in power plants. Thus, proposed plants in the private sector were being set up by new companies. There was no question of their already being a producer of power.

Also, the argument that the captive blocks were to be given to those units that were already producing power does not take into account that, at that time, private investment in power generation had been permitted as a policy only a year earlier. It needed five to six years to set up new power plants. There were very few private power plants earlier, as the sector was under government control. For setting up new units, private players would have to approach the state government for land, water and environment clearances, and would need a coal linkage to decide the size and specification of the power plant. They needed to know the availability of coal through the captive block route to tie up the key parameters and technical specifications of the plant. So if new units had to be set up, they needed the captive block allocation to set up a new plant. To argue that this policy was aimed at benefiting only those few and chosen companies that had power plants for historical reasons from the pre-Independence era is to take a very restrictive view of the legislation. It is difficult to imagine that the legislature passed a law to benefit just three or

---

*http://www.indianlegislation.in/BA/BaActToc.aspx?actid=32304

four players. In any case, the new company, even if owned by pre-Independent power plant owners, setting up a power plant could not claim experience, as it would be a separate legal entity under the Companies Act.

The court also found the process of allocation non-transparent. It held that in different meetings of the coal allocation committee, different norms and policies were being adopted. It also held that there was no arrangement for the allocation of a block to a group of companies and appointing one as a leader to manage the block. It criticized the committee for considering applications even when no presentation was made before it, as directed. It found that there was no comparative merit chart to indicate how the decisions were arrived at. It also criticized certain allocations that were not recommended by the state government or the administrative ministry (of power, steel or industry) or opposed by one or the other.

The court did not consider the facts fully before reaching some of the above findings. In the 1990s, when the economy opened up, there was very little demand for captive coal blocks, as the major consumer, the power sector, was not expanding rapidly. Even after allowing captive mining and relaxing licensing conditions, the growth in the power sector was slow, with very little addition of private power capacities. It was only in 2003, when the licensing conditions were removed and economic growth accelerated, that demand for power shot up. There was a sudden jump in the demand for coal blocks as well. So the guidelines very often had to change keeping in view the ground realities.

Committee System of Governance

In the committee system of governance, views of some or the other players have to be overruled. So if the state government or the administrative ministry or, in rare cases, both, were overruled, it would be wrong to call that a weakness or an irregularity. Similarly, the procedure adopted by the committee to allot one coal block to a number of private players was reflective of the size of the block and its reserves not matching, and hence giving benefit to smaller players too. To say that joint allocation is not contemplated in Section 3(3)(a)(iii) of the CMNA is not correct, as there was no bar in the Act against it. The Act only provided that coal mining of the captive block be done by the user, which was being done, and that the coal that was mined be used for the prescribed purpose under the Act. For this purpose, the block was for captive use of the group of allotees. Similarly, the argument that reasons for rejection were not given in the minutes of the meeting must be seen in the context that there were a large number of applicants and a wide nature of factors to be considered. The committee, therefore, recorded the decisions and did not often give reasons for rejections. The court has not realized that in a committee system of decision-making, the safeguard against any wrong decision is the representation received from those whose applications are rejected. Very few such representations were received.

I recall hundreds of committees chaired by me, and some by eminent people, including SC judges, of which I was a member. I have seen Cabinet meetings. In all these, only the decision of the committee or the Cabinet was recorded. To record detailed minutes can also pose a problem. If, for some reason, during recording of minutes some factor is not mentioned, the decision, if otherwise fair, can be questioned. It is not transparent, but so are practically all committee systems of decision-making. The court, by questioning the system, has not fully appreciated the nature of the committee system of decision-making, its limitations and its safeguards. If the allocations were unfair, there would be a host of representations.

When Boundaries Are Blurred

An important dimension of public governance is involved when we consider the consequences of the decisions taken by the screening committee for coal-block allocation. When does any decision of a public servant cross the boundary of an administrative or judicial act and become a corrupt action liable for criminal punishment? Where does the boundary of an administrative action end and criminality seep in? When do administrative or judicial decisions become corrupt acts?

Let me briefly emphasize the facts that give rise to these issues. As mentioned earlier, the CAG's report had been followed up with a PIL in the SC. Allegations of corruption of huge magnitude based on the loss of revenue mentioned in the CAG report were made. It was alleged that coal blocks had not been given by the screening committee in accordance with the notified policy and since these were given to private players, there was huge loss to the government. It was considered a criminal offence by the CBI liable for punishment under the provisions of the Prevention of Corruption Act, 1988.* The difficulty was that the Act did not

---

*The Prevention of Corruption Act, 1947, was repealed in 1988 and several

distinguish between bona fide and mala fide decisions clearly.

In the government, thousands of decisions are taken at various levels. Very often, circulars are issued to clarify the government's intention on certain issues. Some decisions turn out to be right and others don't. Similarly, in the judicial system, decisions are taken by judges. Many of these are overturned during the appeal. The apex court itself often reviews its own decisions on critical issues. But when decisions are overturned or courts review their decision, we do not consider them corrupt acts. This is because it is an act done in the normal course of business. If, however, there was some indication that money was exchanged for arriving at a judicial decision, it would be considered a corrupt act. Similarly, in the case of other public servants taking decisions on administrative issues, when things are done in the normal course of business and decisions are taken that are in violation of existing administrative instructions, such orders need to be changed. It is somewhat like the judgement of a court overturned by a superior court for the wrong application of law or the improper appreciation of facts. Wrong decisions do not become criminal acts unless there is proof of money exchanging hands or quid pro quo and thus gaining benefit or mala fide action.

This was apparently also the view of the SC earlier in 2007, when the question of irregularities in petrol-pump allocations was involved.

---

important provisions were added to it. This expanded the definition of public servants and put in a detailed provision defining criminal misconduct. Section 13(1)(d)(iii) was also added at that time. This has contributed greatly to the blurring of administrative and corrupt acts. In 2018, the Act has been further amended and Section 13 has been substantially changed.

It is useful to recall the full facts of the case. Petrol pumps had been allotted to various individuals during 2000–02 by public-sector oil companies based on the recommendation of committees. These committees included former judges and oil-company officials. It was alleged that these allotments were done as political patronage. When reports appeared in press in August 2002 and there was criticism in the Parliament, the government decided to cancel all allotments. The matter went to the SC, which decided to form a committee of two retired justices (one from the SC and the other from the High Court) to examine all allotments. Out of more than 400 allotments, three-fourth were found to be against rules or done under political patronage. The SC accepted the recommendations with some modifications and agreed to retain the allotments of a few more persons. But it did not hold that these persons of the selection board must be investigated by the CBI or that criminal proceedings should be launched against them. It was an administrative decision and the court left it at that. This interpretation of the legal framework was not followed in the coal case.

The governance structure will suffer if we do not correct this aberration that has crept in, where we are charging people for criminal misconduct for infringement of administrative circulars. All administrative decisions when reviewed may not necessarily conform to the interpretations of the reviewing authority. If considered necessary, these decisions can be overturned. But for any criminal action or treating any wrong decision as corrupt, there has to be proof of mala fide action and some benefits accruing to the concerned administrative authority who took the decision. If we do not accept this approach and continue with the current strange interpretation of our laws, it will be disastrous for our polity.

(The law has since been changed and some of these concerns have been taken care of in the new 2018 law on corruption.) There is also need for a review of the interpretations of Section 3 of the CMNA for reasons that have been outlined earlier. Who will take the lead?

The events of this period also reflect a strong interplay of the social environment around the institutions of governance and other democratic functionaries. Such interplay invariably changes the narrative. It is well known that corruption in Indian society is high. Part of it can be traced to poverty and low per capita incomes as is the global picture too. But as incomes rise, people expect a more responsible bureaucracy and higher levels of honesty. Given the high level of corruption in the country, civil servants are often seen in that light and their actions become suspect. The several incidents of corruption during this period affected the views of the court, the CAG and the media when taking a view of these developments. There was a great desire to attack corruption. So benefits to industry or the private sector were considered unholy and criticized. The economic logic of the original decision taken on these issues was lost. The government only strengthened the belief that all was not well with its decision on licensing to telecom players in a manner that was open to question and dragging its feet on the issue of introducing captive mining in coal by the competitive-bidding route.

There is also a larger question involved here. Under our Constitution, different arms, namely the Parliament, the executive and the judiciary, have clearly demarcated powers. The national auditor, or the CAG, has a clear mandate under its act. But when institutions start treading on each others' toes, our system will be rocked. Whether driven by the zeal to identify corrupt acts or to clean the system or for some other laudable motive, each institution must not move beyond its boundaries. The period between 2007 and 2014 was turbulent, which saw institutions crossing into the domain of the executive. In its two reports on coal and telecom, the CAG assumed the role of the government's economic policymaker and computed losses. This was a disastrous approach and against all norms of governance.

There is an argument that the government should have revised the spectrum charges in 2007 and that the private captive block owners should have been deprived of their comparative advantage as against other players. Possibly, there is some merit in these arguments. The auditors or the courts could point out, criticize and suggest policies, but it is an unhealthy democratic convention to start laying down government policies. This not only had a massive adverse impact on the system of governance but also huge adverse repercussions on the morale of the civil services, especially when the CAG reports were followed up with criminal cases.

EPILOGUE

On a winter afternoon in 2010 a special secretary of the MHA called to inform me that the President had approved the Padma Bhushan for my outstanding work in the field of public administration. He wanted to know if I would accept the award. I indicated my acceptance.

For three years, I had chaired the committee that makes recommendation for these awards to the PM. But now that I was out of the system, I had no inkling of impending decisions. I marvelled at the ability of the government to maintain secrecy where they wished to. Normally, the ship of the state leaks heavily from the top!

Receiving the third-highest civilian award of the country was indeed a signal honour. I got confirmation of the final decision when I saw my name mentioned in the list of persons on whom the award had been conferred, published in the newspapers on 26 January 2010. The actual ceremony for the conferment of the award was held in Rashtrapati Bhawan, Delhi, in late March that year.

Over the years, as I have reflected on the functioning of the government systems, several issues worry me. I am convinced, and so are perhaps a vast majority of our citizens, that we cannot become a modern, developed nation with high per capita incomes and low levels of corruption, unless we bring major reforms in our system of governance. If India has to become the largest economy in the world by 2050, our governance structure has to be reformed in a major way. This I would consider a necessary condition, but not sufficient. Our economic growth will substantially be determined by our economic policies. But good governance will enable faster development and more efficient use of resources. Let me indicate some critical areas, several of which I have alluded to briefly in various chapters earlier flowing directly from my experience.

Strong Institutions Need Committed Individuals

A democracy requires well-functioning, strong institutions. It needs traditions and norms evolved over long years when we consider appointment to some key institutions of governance. These processes must inspire confidence in people. I have already argued earlier the need for an institutional arrangement for the appointment of Cabinet secretary. He is the highest-ranking civil servant in the country, and transparency and fairness in civil-service appointments must be reflected in his selection. The office of the CAG is another key institution. It audits government expenses, revenues and has a thorough look at the effective use of government money for the welfare of the people. The government's accountability to its people is strengthened by its reports. The current system of selection of the CAG is wholly non-transparent and dependent upon politicians. Similarly, the chief election commissioner (CEC) and election commissioners are appointed through a non-transparent selection process. Members of the Union Public Service Commission (UPSC) are also being selected without any well-laid-out evaluation process.

My experience over the years has been that these have become political selections, with very little transparency or institutional arrangement for the decisions. I recall I would find decisions regarding the selection of UPSC members kept pending for no apparent reason. When I would get it one fine morning from the PMO, I would still be unclear on how it had been done. In one case, a prospective member came to me requesting an expeditious decision regarding a service matter related to her so that she could be appointed a member of the UPSC. And she was later appointed as one. Since these are key constitutional offices, we must have a short list prepared by senior-level civil servants, academicians or other qualified persons. It is no use involving the CJI or the leader of the Opposition if the panel of candidates is not of the best quality. The final selection must be done in consultation with the leader of the Opposition in the Lok Sabha and the Rajya Sabha, and a representative of the CJI. Ultimately, however, it is the holders of these offices who will bring greater credibility to the institutions by their fair and just functioning. The moral side of civil servants needs to come out strongly in these jobs. The selection process must consider this a key requirement.

A good governance structure will require officials working for two to three years in any assignment and be accountable for results. Coalition governments are increasingly more in evidence in the last two decades. In the initial four decades, there was single-party dominance at the national level and in many states. Now both at the Centre and in several states, there are coalitions that are in power. In the coming years, the instability inherent in coalitions and the desire to cling to political power may result in unreasonable demands on the administration. The pulls and pressures of transferring civil servants and the politicization of the service may increase. The services are already suffering from major weaknesses. The conduct of an increasing number of civil servants is not upright, fair and honest. There is a lot of corruption among them and many are willing to do the unlawful bidding of political masters.

This downslide has to stop.

We need a model code for civil servants and politicians that encompasses many of these issues and promotes a clean and accountable administration. The officers who help politicians collect money for their parties or for their personal expenses, or lose their ability to work independently will need to be identified. In case of gross violation, officers guilty of such infringement need to be compulsorily retired, and politicians debarred from participating in the electoral process for a minimum of three years. We may need a new law on civil service and changes in electoral law for this. We can start with an ombudsman overseeing this process of long tenures and adherence to the code at the Centre and in some states, to begin with. This must be done on mission mode.

It is extremely important to promote probity in the public life of ministers and secretaries to the government. At present, this function is not specifically allocated. With expanding gift culture and corruption, a close monitoring is required. We need to see whether the members of the Council of Ministers and secretaries are adhering to the code of conduct prescribed to them. Since the PM and the CMs must keep a close watch on their conduct, this function needs to be done. Earlier I have suggested that the Cabinet secretary should undertake this function. For the states, the chief secretary could oversee violations of the code. In case of violations, in the first instance, this should be pointed out to the minister or the secretary concerned. Once the misconduct has been brought out in this manner, the level of compliance with norms of probity is likely to improve.

Money, Power and Politics

During my years with the government, particularly in the last two decades, I have observed that regional parties reflecting the aspirations of their respective states are now quite powerful. While the initial four decades saw the Congress in most states, its say is now weak. The BJP, which emerged as a powerful force in 2014, may not have a similar strength in the coming years. The electoral process is likely to throw up more hung assemblies and the need for a coalition government. The misuse of Article 356 of the Constitution has been kept partly in check by the amendments in the Tenth Schedule of the Constitution, which severely restricted defection and the ruling of the SC in the Bommai case* on inviting parties to form a government.

But there are two issues that still plague the system. First, in the event that there is no clear mandate in an election, a coalition is formed. In such a situation, there is always talk of MLAs being purchased and big financial transactions taking place while a majority is being cobbled. That a group is able to prove majority in the legislative Assembly, in whatever manner possible, is considered adequate by courts. This approach is likely to lead to big money

---

*The SC's landmark judgement in the S.R. Bommai vs Union of India case (1994) sharply limited the constitutional power vested in the Central government to dismiss a state government under Article 356 of the Constitution. It held that this power was subject to judicial review. It can be challenged on the grounds that action was mala fide. Objective material must exist to show that governance cannot be carried on in accordance with provisions of the Constitution.

determining which party will form the government and also to a high prise tag on MLAs for support. A government which starts in this manner will have corruption inbuilt in its constitution. Second, elections are becoming costly affairs, and political funding is a likely source of corruption. The recent introduction of electoral bonds is opaque, and people and the press, who are watchdogs of democracy, have no idea of the source of these funds.

These are complex issues and have no easy solution. We can, however, take measures to minimize the role of money power in our democracy. We must think of the government funding of elections and about bringing transparency to donations to political parties.

Effective governance in the coming years will require further strengthening of the Tenth Schedule of our Constitution. I would suggest a complete ban on defection. Also, where the whole party changes its major coalition partner to get into government, its members should not be allowed to be part of any Cabinet for two years. This will disincentivize defection.

Areas of Reform

A major objective of improving governance is efficient public-service-delivery institutions and a low level of corruption. It has to be realized that abolishing corrupt behaviour is difficult in any country. This is the global experience. But we can sharply reduce it. This requires systemic change. The rules need to be made simpler, and large-scale and efficient use of IT must bring automaticity to the services to be provided to the common man. A lot of work has been done by simplifying the rules related to the ease of doing business. The states are now much more sensitized. But this must be the recurrent theme in states and the Centre. To drive this change, a continuous and long-term effort with a dedicated reform group (I would call it the R Group) in the office of the PM and the CMs must be set up. The group must look at various reform ideas to improve governance and must work on both reforms and implementation. It must be properly staffed with members drawn from IIMs, IITs, the field of IT, the judiciary, the police, the civil services and banking, including economists, and work alongside concerned departments to drive change. It should not indulge in the luxury of report-writing over long periods but must develop ideas, implement them in selected areas and, after assessing results, expand them.

Though aimed at reducing corruption, the objective should not be to discourage risk-taking or to promote inaction by public servants. The government must aim to catch those who give benefits to private parties through the use of their public offices to make money or obtain advantages from them in return. Mere infringement of any government order does not constitute corruption, unless there is mala fide action in it. I notice that both investigating agencies and courts are now often taking any violation of government policy as a corrupt act. This is a harmful approach to reducing corruption. Government officials, quasi-judicial bodies or even courts pass hundreds of orders. There could be a bona fide mistake or difference in view in interpretation of rules, laws or government orders. But unless there is proof of deliberate mischief to obtain personal gain, it is not a corrupt act. This will only promote inaction and lack of risk-taking among civil servants, which is detrimental to any developing nation. We are removing the distinction between an honest officer and a corrupt one if the current interpretation of the law continues. Recent amendments in the anti-corruption law have, however, taken an important step in resolving some of these concerns.

An important area of reform is investment by private-sector players, which is key to faster economic growth. A lot of this investment may be in PPP mode. Institutional arrangements to deal with various eventualities and delays for want of land or a change in government policies when such projects are implemented need to be in place. A large percentage of NPAs of banks are because of our failure to resolve such issues and restructure projects.

In a democracy, institutions must work in accordance with the Constitution and the boundaries that have evolved over time. Recent trends in this regard are worrying. The courts, the CAG and the government have all tried to work beyond their mandates. There has been an increasing number of PILs resulting in the disruption of the court's normal functioning. Cases that should have been disposed of have taken a back seat as the hearings on PILs have taken precedence. The courts have also encroached on the functions of the executive. Imagine the courts running the Board of Control for Cricket in India (BCCI) and having a team to seal buildings in Delhi for violation of the master plan. On the environment, there has been a spate of orders. Policy on the nursery admission of children has been considered umpteen times by the courts. The executive, in recent times, has made efforts to have a decisive say in the appointment of judges. All the above trends are worrisome. Unless institutions work within their boundaries, we will see friction, a weakening of democracy and eventual chaos in the system.

While improving governance systems, we must address the important issue of widespread income inequalities in the country, both inter- and intra-state. There is a large disparity in per capita incomes among states. The ratio between the highest and the lowest incomes continues to be 1:5. Bihar, UP, Jharkhand, Madhya Pradesh, Rajasthan, Assam and Odisha are states with income far below the national average. Again, within many states, there are poorer backward areas with poor health and education indicators. We need an institution working on these, and a host of other national issues, to whom the states and the ministries will pay attention. The Planning Commission, instead of being abolished, should have been reformed. But now that we have a new institution, it should not remain a mere think tank. It must have financial resources at its disposal to allocate funds and address these pressing problems.

India's commitment to climate change requires the development of hydel-power capacities and gas-based plants. We need an effective policy, especially for the development of hydel power in Arunachal Pradesh. While developing such plants, we will have to maintain and protect our biodiversity and look at how best to conserve the water we are using. I would suggest that a minimum amount of water must flow in the riverbed at all times. There are a number of gas-based power capacities lying idle, producing only NPAs of banks. A lot of natural gas produced by the ONGC is being given to fertilizer plants. This has to change. We must ensure a minimum 50 per cent capacity utilization of these power plants for five years, during which most of the bank loan can be repaid. Gas produced by the ONGC should be given to gas-based plants during this period. The fertilizer plants could run on LNG, which is being imported. This may increase government financial support to fertilizer plants, but it will reduce NPAs, which will save public money. These plants will generate clean power and reduce pollution. These will also ensure uninterrupted renewable energy, say, in the night or when the sun's energy is not available; these could supplement renewable-energy

209

plants which give infirm power. Coal-based plants are less suitable for this, as gas-based capacities can be ramped up quickly.

While I have alluded to some areas of reform, there are others on which similar work needs to be done. The position in states is precarious. The delivery of health and education services is poor. Our judicial system is clogged and people do not get justice for years, even while running from one court to another. The police is still poorly staffed as compared to international norms and does not inspire confidence in the common man. The commitment to strengthening democratic institutions is still not strong in all governments. There is a perception that the governments are trying to exercise control over the functioning of some key institutions of democracy, such as the media, the Election Commission of India (ECI), the Reserve Bank of India (RBI), the CBI, the University Grants Commission (UGC) and the universities. This approach is regressive and harmful for the growth of any democracy. We need to develop strong autonomous institutions manned by individuals of intellectual integrity.

In May 1967, Nobel Prize-winning author Alexander Solzhenitsyn, while talking about literature that was being churned out at that time, had warned writers in the former Soviet Union that 'literature that is not the breath of contemporary society, that dares not transmit the pains and fears of that society, that does not warn in time against threatening moral and social dangers—such literature does not deserve the name of literature; it is only a façade. Such literature loses the confidence of its own people, and its published works are used as wastepaper instead of being read.'

Our governance reforms must be the 'breath of contemporary society', must address its 'pains' and deal with 'moral and social dangers'. This alone will make us a great power on the global scene.

ACKNOWLEDGEMENTS

I am thankful to a number of people who have been very generous with their comments and views about the events of that time. Since I have never kept a detailed record of official events, I had to depend heavily on published sources. Among those who helped me with their observations on some events, I would like to make particular mention of Dhirendra Singh, former home secretary; Neelam Sabharwal, former high commissioner in Cyprus; and M. Damodaran, former chairman of SEBI. Montek Singh Ahluwalia, the former deputy chairman of the Planning Commission, was very generous with his detailed comments on certain issues. Alok Perti, the former coal secretary, took great pains and presented me with his views, which helped me a great deal. I would especially like to thank my wife Vibha, who has been very patient while I have worked on this book. I am grateful to the team at Rupa Publications for their wholehearted support and enthusiasm.

I hope this effort will encourage more of my colleagues to write and add to the growing literature on issues of public governance.

INDEX

INDEX

INDEX